Michael Moorcock is astonishing. His enormous output includes around fifty novels, innumerable short stories and a rock album. Born in London in 1939, he became editor of *Tarzan Adventures* at sixteen, moving on later to edit the *Sexton Blake Library*. He has earned his living as a writer/editor ever since, and is without doubt one of Britain's most popular and most prolific authors. He has been compared with Tennyson, Tolkien, Raymond Chandler, Wyndham Lewis, Ronald Firbank, Mervyn Peake, Edgar Allan Poe, Colin Wilson, Anatole France, William Burroughs, Edgar Rice Burroughs, Charles Dickens, James Joyce, Vladimir Nabokov, Jorge Luis Borges, Joyce Cary, Ray Bradbury, H. G. Wells, George Bernard Shaw and Hieronymus Bosch, among others.

'No one at the moment in England is doing more to break down the artificial divisions that have grown up in novel writing – realism, surrealism, science fiction, historical fiction, social satire, the poetic novel – than Michael Moorcock.'
Angus Wilson

'He is an ingenious and energetic experimenter, restlessly original, brimming over with clever ideas.'
Robert Nye, *The Guardian*

Michael Moorcock

The Runestaff

The History of the Runestaff

Volume Four

A MAYFLOWER BOOK

GRANADA
London Toronto Sydney New York

Published by Granada Publishing Limited
in 1969
Reprinted 1969, 1973 (twice), 1974, 1975, 1977, 1980

ISBN 0 583 11499 7

Granada Publishing Limited
Frogmore, St Albans, Herts AL2 2NF
and
3 Upper James Street, London W1R 4BP
866 United Nations Plaza, New York, NY 10017, USA
117 York Street, Sydney, NSW 2000, Australia
100 Skyway Avenue, Rexdale, Ontario, M9W 3A6, Canada
PO Box 84165, Greenside, 2034 Johannesburg, South Africa
61 Beach Road, Auckland, New Zealand

Made and printed in Great Britain by
Hunt Barnard Printing Ltd.,
Aylesbury, Bucks.
Set in Intertype Times

Granada ®
Granada Publishing ®

To Jim Cawthorn, who helped create these

Contents

BOOK ONE

CHAPTER ONE

AN EPISODE IN KING HUON'S THRONE ROOM

Tacticians and Warriors of ferocious courage and skill; careless of their own lives; corrupt of soul and mad of brain; haters of all that was not in decay; wielders of power without morality—force without justice; the Barons of Granbretan carried the standard of their King Emperor Huon across the continent of Europe and made that continent their property, carried the banner to West and East to other continents to which they also laid claim. And it seemed that no force, either natural or supernatural, was strong enough to halt the insane and deadly tide.

Indeed, none now resisted them at all. With chuckling pride and cold contempt they demanded whole nations as tribute and the tribute was paid.

In all the subdued lands few hoped. Of those, fewer dared express their hope—and among those few hardly a single soul possessed the courage to murmur the name symbolising that hope.

The name was Castle Brass.

Those who spoke the name understood its implications, for Castle Brass was the only stronghold that remained unvanquished by the warlords of Granbretan and Castle Brass housed heroes; men who had fought the Dark Empire, whose names were loathed and hated by the brooding Baron Meliadus, Grand Constable of the Order of the Wolf, Commander of the Army of Conquest, for it was

9

known that Baron Meliadus fought a private
feud with those heroes, particularly the legendary Dorian Hawkmoon von Köln who was
married to the woman Meliadus desired,
Yisselda, daughter of Count Brass of Castle
Brass.

But Castle Brass had not defeated the armies
of Granbretan, it had merely evaded them, disappearing by means of a strange, ancient crystal
machine into another dimension of the Earth,
where those heroes, Hawkmoon, Count Brass,
Huillam D'Averc, Oladahn of the Bulgar
Mountains and their handful of Kamargian
men-at-arms, now sheltered, and most folk felt
that the heroes of the Kamarg had deserted
them forever. They did not blame them, but
their hope waned fainter with every day that
passed and the heroes did not return.

In that other Kamarg, sundered from its
original by mysterious dimension of time and
space, Hawkmoon and the rest were faced with
fresh problems, for it seemed that the sorcerer-
scientists of the Dark Empire were close to
discovering means either of breaking through
into their dimension or of recalling them. The
enigmatic Warrior in Jet and Gold had advised
Hawkmoon and D'Averc to go on a quest to a
strange new land to seek the legendary Sword
of the Dawn, which would be of aid to them in
their struggle, and which would in turn aid
The Runestaff, which, the Warrior insisted,
Hawkmoon served. Having won the rosy sword,
Hawkmoon was then informed he must travel
by sea around the coast of Amarehk to the city
of Dnark, where the services of the blade were
required. But Hawkmoon demurred. He was
anxious to return to the Kamarg and see his
beautiful wife Yisselda again. In a ship supplied
by Bewchard of Narleen, Hawkmoon set sail
for Europe, against the dictates of the
Warrior in Jet and Gold who had told him that
his duty to The Runestaff, that mysterious arte-

10

*fact said to control all human destinies, was
greater than his duty to his wife, friends and
adopted homeland. With the foppish Huillam
D'Averc by his side, Hawkmoon headed out to
sea.*

*Meanwhile in Granbretan Baron Meliadus
fumed at what he considered his King-
Emperor's foolishness in not allowing him to
pursue his vendetta against Castle Brass. When
Shenegar Trott, Count of Sussex, seemed to be
favoured over him by a King-Emperor growing
steadily more mistrustful of his unstable con-
quistador, Meliadus became rebellious, pursuing
his prey to the Wastes of Yel, losing them, and
returning with redoubled hatred to Londra,
there to scheme not only against the heroes
of Castle Brass, but also against his immortal
ruler, Huon, the King-Emperor . . .*

—The High History of the Runestaff

THE VAST DOORS parted and Baron Meliadus, but
lately returned from Yel, walked into the throne room
of his King-Emperor, to report his failures and his
discoveries.

As Meliadus entered the hall, whose roof seemed so
tall as to be one with the heavens and whose walls were
so distant as to seem to encompass an entire country,
his way was blocked by a double line of guards. These
guards, members of the King Emperor's own Order of
the Mantis and wearing the great jewelled insect-masks
belonging to that Order, seemed reluctant to let him
pass through.

Meliadus controlled himself with difficulty and waited
while the ranks drew back to admit him.

Then he strode into the hall of blazing colour, whose
galleries were hung with the gleaming banners of Granbretan's five hundred greatest families and whose walls
were encrusted with a mosaic of precious gems depicting
Granbretan's might and history, along an aisle made up
on either side by a thousand mantis warriors, each statue-
still, towards the Throne Globe more than a mile distant,

Half-way to the Globe, he abased himself in a somewhat peremptory fashion.

The solid black sphere seemed to shudder momentarily as Baron Meliadus rose, then the black became shot through with veins of scarlet and white which slowly spread through the darker shade until it had vanished altogether. The mixture like milk and blood swirled and cleared to reveal a tiny foetus-like shape curled in the centre of the sphere. From this twisted figure peered eyes that were hard, black and sharp, containing an old—indeed, an immortal—intelligence. This was Huon, King Emperor of Granbretan and the Dark Empire, Grand Constable of the Order of the Mantis, wielder of absolute power over tens of millions of souls, the ruler who would live forever and in whose name Baron Meliadus had conquered the whole of Europe and beyond.

The voice of a golden youth now issued from the Throne Globe (the golden youth to whom it had belonged had been dead a thousand years):

" Ah, our impetuous Baron Meliadus . . ."

Again Meliadus bowed and murmured. " Your servant, Prince of All."

" And what have you to report to us, hasty lord? "

" Success, Great Emperor. Proof of my suspicions . . ."

" You have found the missing emissaries from Asiacommunista? "

" I regret not, Noble Sire . . ."

Baron Meliadus did not know that it had been in this disguise that Hawkmoon and D'Averc had penetrated the capital of the Dark Empire. Only Flana Mikosevaar, who had helped them escape, knew that.

" Then why are you here, baron? "

" I discovered that Hawkmoon, whom I insist is still the greatest threat to our security, has been visiting our island. I went to Yel and there found him and the traitor Huillam D'Averc, as well as the magician Mygan of Llandar. They know the secret of travelling through the dimensions." Baron Meliadus did not mention that they had escaped from him. " Before we could apprehend them, they vanished before our eyes. Mighty Monarch, if they can come and go from our land at will, surely it is plain that we can never be safe until they are destroyed,

12

I would suggest we begin immediately to direct all the efforts of our scientists—of Taragorm and Kalan in particular—to finding these renegades and finishing them. They threaten us from within . . ."

"Baron Meliadus. What news of the emissaries from Asiacommunista? "

"None, so far, Mighty King Emperor, but . . ."

"A few guerillas, Baron Meliadus, this empire may contend with, but if our shores are threatened by a force as great, if not greater, than our own, by a force, moreover that is possessed of scientific secrets unknown to us, that we may not survive, you see , , ." The golden voice spoke with acid patience.

Meliadus frowned. "We have no proof that such an invasion is planned, Monarch of the World . . ."

"Agreed. Neither have we proof, Baron Meliadus, that Hawkmoon and his band of terrorists have the power to do us any great harm." Streaks of ice blue suddenly appeared in the Throne Globe's fluid.

"Great King Emperor. Give me the time and the resources , . ."

"We are an expanding empire, Baron Meliadus. We wish to expand still further. It would be pessimistic, would it not, to stand still? That is not our way. We are proud of our influence upon the Earth. We wish to extend it. You seem uneager to carry out the principles of our ambition which is to spread a great, laughing terror to the corners of the world. You are becoming small-minded, we fear . . ."

"But by refusing to counter those subtle forces that might wreck our schemes, Prince of All, we could betray our destiny also!"

"We resent dissension, Baron Meliadus. Your personal hatred of Hawkmoon and, we have heard, your desire for Yisselda of Brass, represent dissension. We have your self-interest at heart, baron, for if you continue in this course, we shall be obliged to elect another over you, to dismiss you from our service—aye, even to dismiss you from your Order . . ."

Instinctively, Baron Meliadus's gauntleted hands leapt fearfully to his mask. *To be unmasked!* The greatest disgrace—the greatest horror of them all! For that was

13

what the threat implied. To join the ranks of the lowest scum in Londra—the caste of the unmasked ones! Meliadus shuddered and could hardly bring himself to speak.

At last he murmured. " I will reflect on your words, Emperor of the Earth . . ."

" Do so, Baron Meliadus. We would not wish to see such a great conqueror destroyed by a few clouded thoughts. If you would regain all our favour, you will find for us the means by which the Asiacommunistan emissaries left."

Baron Meliadus fell to his knees, his great wolf-mask nodding, his arms outspread. Thus the conqueror of Europe abased himself before his Lord, but his brain flared with a dozen rebellious thoughts and he thanked the spirit of his Order that the mask hid his face so that his fury did not show.

He backed away from the Throne Globe while the beady, sardonic eyes of the King Emperor regarded him. Huon's prehensile tongue darted out to touch a jewel floating near the shrunken head and the milky fluid swirled, ·flashed with rainbow colours, then gradually turned black once more.

Meliadus wheeled and began the long march back to the gigantic doors, feeling that every eye behind the unmoving mantis masks watched him with malevolent humour.

When he had passed through the doors, he turned to the left and strode through the corridors of the twisted palace, seeking the apartments of the Countess Flana Mikosevaar of Kanbery, widow of Asrovak Mikosevaar, the Muskovian renegade who had once headed the Vulture Legion. Countess Flana not only was now titular head of the Vulture Legion, but also cousin to the King Emperor —his only surviving kin.

CHAPTER TWO

HUMAN THOUGHTS OF THE COUNTESS FLANA

THE HERON MASK of spun gold lay on the lacquered table before her as she stared through the window, over the curling, crazy spires of the city of Londra, her pale, beautiful face full of sadness and confusion.

As she moved, the rich silks and jewels of her gown caught the light from the red sun. She went to a closet and opened it. There were the strange costumes she had kept since those two visitors had left her apartments so many days before. The disguises that Hawkmoon and D'Averc had used when posing as princes from Asiacommunista. Now she wondered where they were—particularly D'Averc whom she knew loved her.

Flana, Countess of Kanbery, had had a dozen husbands and more lovers, had disposed of them in one way or another as a woman might dispose of a useless pair of stockings. She had never known love, never had the feelings of emotion known to most others, even the rulers of Granbretan.

But somehow D'Averc, that dandified renegade who claimed to be permanently ill, had aroused these feelings in her. Perhaps she had remained so remote heretofore because she was sane, while those surrounding her at court were not, because she was gentle and capable of selfless love, whereas the lords of the Dark Empire understood nothing of such feelings. Perhaps D'Averc, gentle, subtle, sensitive, had awakened her from an apathy induced not by lack of soul, but by a greatness of soul—such greatness that it could not bear to exist in the mad, selfish, perverse world of the Court of King Huon.

But now that the Countess Flana was awake, she could not ignore the horror of her surroundings, the despair she felt that her lover of a single night might never return, that he might even be already dead.

She had taken to her apartments, avoiding contact with the rest, but while this ruse afforded her some surcease from understanding of her circumstances, it only allowed her sorrow silence in which to grow.

Tears fell down Flana's perfect cheeks and she stopped their flow with a scented silken scarf.

A maidservant entered the room and hesitated on the threshold. Automatically Flana reached for her heron mask.

"What is it?"

"The Baron Meliadus of Kroiden, my lady. He says he has to speak with you. A matter of paramount urgency."

Flana slipped her mask over her head and settled it on her shoulders.

She considered the girl's words for a moment and then shrugged. What did it matter if she saw Meliadus for a few moments? Perhaps he had some news of D'Averc, whom she knew he hated. By subtle means she might discover what he knew.

But what if Meliadus wished to make love to her, as he had on previous occasions?

Why, she would turn him away, as she had turned him away before.

She inclined the lovely heron mask a fraction.

"Admit the baron," she said.

CHAPTER THREE

HAWKMOON ALTERS HIS COURSE

THE GREAT SAILS curved in the wind as the ship sped over the surface of the sea. The sky was clear and the sea was calm, a vast expanse of azure. Oars had been shipped and the helmsman now looked to the main deck for his course. The bosun, clad in orange and black, climbed to the deck where Hawkmoon stood staring across the ocean.

Hawkmoon's golden hair streamed in the wind and his cloak of wine-coloured velvet whipped out behind him. His handsome features were battle-hardened and weather beaten and were only marred by the existence, embedded in his forehead, of a dull, black stone. Gravely, he acknowledged the bosun's salute.

"I've given orders to sail around the coast, heading due East, sir," the bosun said.

"Who gave you that course, bosun?"

"Why, nobody, sir. I just assumed that since we were heading for Dnark . . ."

"We are not heading for Dnark, tell the helmsman."

"But that strange warrior—the Warrior in Jet and Gold you called him—he said . . ."

"He is not my master, bosun. No—we sail out to sea now. For Europe."

"For Europe, sir! You know that after you saved Narleen we would take you anywhere, follow you anywhere, but have you any understanding of the distances we must sail to reach Europe—the seas we should have to cross, the storms . . .?"

"Aye, I understand. But we still sail for Europe."

"As you say, sir." Frowning, the bosun turned away to give his orders to the helmsman.

From his cabin below the main deck, D'Averc now emerged and began to climb the ladder. Hawkmoon grinned at him. "Did you sleep well, friend D'Averc?"

"As well as possible aboard this rocking tub. I am

inclined to suffer from insomnia at the best of times, Hawkmoon, but I snatched a few moments. The best, I suppose, I may expect."

Hawkmoon laughed. "When I looked in on you an hour ago, you were snoring."

D'Averc raised his eyebrows. "So! You heard me breathing heavily, eh? I tried to keep as quiet as possible, but this cold of mine—contracted since coming aboard—is giving me a certain amount of difficulty." He raised a tiny square of linen to the tip of his nose.

D'Averc was dressed in silk, with a loose blue shirt, flowing scarlet breeks, a heavy broad leather belt supporting his sword and a dirk. Around his bronzed throat was wound a long scarf of purple and his long hair was held back by a band that matched his breeks. His fine, almost ascetic features, bore their usual sardonic expression.

"Did I hear aright below?" D'Averc asked. "Were you instructing the bosun to head for Europe?"

"I was."

"So you still intend to try to reach Castle Brass and forget what the Warrior in Jet and Gold said of your destiny—that it was to take that blade there," now D'Averc pointed at the great red broadsword at Hawkmoon's side, "to Dnark, there to serve the Runestaff?"

"I owe allegiance to myself and my kin before I will serve an artefact in whose existence I gravely doubt."

"You would not have believed before in the powers of that blade, the Sword of the Dawn," D'Averc remarked wryly, "yet you saw it summon warriors from thin air to save our lives."

An obstinate look passed over Hawkmoon's features. "Aye," he agreed reluctantly. "But I still intend to return to Castle Brass, if that is possible."

"There's no telling if it's in this dimension or another."

"I know that also. I can only hope that it is in this dimension." Hawkmoon spoke with finality, showing his unwillingness to discuss the matter further. D'Averc raised his eyebrows for a second time, then descended to the deck and strolled along it whistling.

For five days they sailed on through the calm ocean, every sail unfurled to give them maximum speed.

On the sixth day the bosun came up to Hawkmoon, who was standing in the prow of the ship, and pointed ahead.

"See the dark sky on the horizon, sir. A storm of some sort and we're heading straight for it."

Hawkmoon peered in the direction the bosun indicated. "A storm, you say. Yet it has a peculiar look to it."

"Aye, sir. Shall I reef the sails?"

"No, bosun. We sail on until we have a better idea of what we are heading into."

"As you say, sir." The bosun walked back down the deck, shaking his head.

A few hours later the sky ahead took on the appearance of a lurid wall that stretched across the sea from horizon to horizon, its predominant colours dark red and purple. It towered upwards and yet the sky above them was as blue as it ever had been and the sea was perfectly calm. Only the wind had dropped slightly. It was as if they sailed in a lake, whose banks rose on all sides to disappear into the heavens. The crew was disconcerted and there was a note of fear in the bosun's voice when he next confronted Hawkmoon.

"Do we sail on, sir? I have never heard of such a thing as this before, never experienced anything like it. The crew's nervous, sir, and I'll admit that I am, also."

Hawkmoon nodded sympathetically. "It's peculiar, right enough, seeming to be more supernatural than natural."

"That's what the crew's saying, sir."

Hawkmoon's own instinct was to press on and face whatever it was, but he had a responsibility to the crew, each member of which had volunteered to sail with him in gratitude for his ridding their home city, Narleen, of the power of the Pirate Lord, Valjon of Starvel, previous owner of the Sword of the Dawn.

Hawkmoon sighed. "Very well, bosun. We'll take in all sail and wait the night. With luck, the phenomenon will have passed by morning."

The bosun was relieved. "Thank you, sir."

Hawkmoon acknowledged his salute then turned to stare up at the huge walls. Were they cloud or were they something else? A chill had come into the air and although the sun still shone down, its rays did not seem to touch the lurid walls.

All was still. Hawkmoon wondered if he had made a wise decision in heading away from Dnark. None, to his knowledge, save the ancients had ever sailed these oceans. Who was to tell what uncharted terrors inhabited them?

Night fell, and in the distance the vast, lurid walls could still be seen, their dark reds and purples piercing the blackness of the night. And yet the colours hardly seemed to have the usual properties of light.

Hawkmoon began to feel perturbed.

In the morning the walls seemed to have drawn in much closer and the area of blue sea seemed much smaller. Hawkmoon wondered if they had not been caught in some strange trap, set by giants or some supernatural agencies.

Clad in a thick cloak that did not keep out much of the chill, he paced the deck at dawn.

D'Averc was next to emerge, wearing at least three cloaks and shivering ostentatiously. "A fresh morning, Hawkmoon."

"Aye," murmured the Duke of Köln. "What do you make of it, D'Averc?"

The Frenchman shook his head. "It's a grim sort of stuff, isn't it? Here comes the bosun."

They both turned to greet the bosun. He, too, was wrapped up heavily in a great leather cloak normally used for protection when sailing through a storm.

"Any thoughts on this, bosun?" D'Averc asked.

The bosun shook his head and addressed Hawkmoon. "The men say that whatever happens, sir, they are yours. They will die in your service if necessary."

"They're in a gloomy mood, I gather," smiled D'Averc. "Well, who's to blame them?"

"Who indeed, sir." The bosun's round, honest face looked despairing. "Shall I give the order to sail on, sir?"

"It would be better than waiting here while the stuff closes in," Hawkmoon said. "Let go the sails, bosun."

The bosun shouted orders and men began to climb

through the rigging, letting down the sails and securing their lines. Gradually the sails filled and the ship began to move, seemingly reluctantly, towards the strange cliffs of cloud.

Yet even as they moved forward, the cliffs began to swirl and become agitated. Other, darker colours crept in and a wailing noise drifted towards the ship from all sides. The crew could barely contain its panic, many men standing frozen in the rigging as they watched. Hawkmoon peered forward anxiously.

Then, instantly, the walls had vanished!

Hawkmoon gasped.

Calm sea lay on all sides. Everything was as before. The crew began to cheer, but Hawkmoon noticed that D'Averc's face was bleak. Hawkmoon, too, felt that perhaps the danger was not past. He waited, poised at the rail.

Then from the sea erupted a huge beast.

The crew's cheers changed to screams of fear.

Other beasts began to emerge all around them. Gigantic, reptilian monsters with gaping red jaws and triple rows of teeth, the water streaming from their scales and their blazing eyes full of mad, rolling evil.

There was a deafening flapping noise and one by one the giant reptiles climbed into the air.

"We are done for, Hawkmoon," said D'Averc philosophically as he drew his sword. "It's a pity not to have had one last sight of Castle Brass, nor one last kiss from the lips of those women we love."

Hawkmoon barely heard him. He was full of bitterness at the fate which had decided that he should meet his end in this wet and lonely place, that none would know where or how he had died . . .

CHAPTER FOUR

ORLAND FANK

THE SHADOWS OF the gigantic beasts swept back and forth over the deck and the noise of their wings filled the air. Hawkmoon looked upwards in cold detachment as a monster descended, its maw distended and the Duke of Köln prepared himself in the knowledge that his life had ended. But then the monster had flapped skyward again, having snapped once at the high mast.

Nerves tense, muscles taut, Dorian Hawkmoon drew the Sword of the Dawn, the blade which no other man could wield and live. But he knew that even his supernatural broadsword would be useless against the dreadful beasts; knew that they need not even attack the crew directly, that they need only strike the ship a few blows to send those aboard to the bottom.

The ship rocked in the wind created by the vast wings and the air stank of their foetid breath.

D'Averc frowned. "Why are they not attacking? Are they playing a game with us?"

"It seems likely," nodded Hawkmoon, speaking between clenched teeth. "Maybe it pleases them to play with us for a while before destroying us."

As a great shadow descended, D'Averc leapt up and slashed at a beast with his sword but the creature had flapped up into the air again before D'Averc's feet returned to the deck. He wrinkled his nose. "Ugh! The stink! It can do my lungs no good."

Now, one by one, each of the creatures descended and struck the ship a few thwacks with their leathery wings. The ship shuddered and men screamed as they were flung from the rigging to the deck. Hawkmoon and D'Averc staggered, clinging to the rail to save themselves from toppling.

"They're turning the ship!" D'Averc cried in puzzlement. "We're being forced round!"

Hawkmoon stared grimly at the terrifying monsters and said nothing. Soon the ship had been swung round by about eighty degrees and then the beasts rose higher into the sky and wheeled above the ship as if debating their next action. Hawkmoon looked at their eyes, trying to discern intelligence there, trying to discover some hint of their intentions, but it was impossible.

And then the creatures began to flap away until they were far to sternward. And then they began to turn again.

In formation the beasts flapped their wings until such a wind was created that Hawkmoon and D'Averc could no longer keep their footing and they were pressed down to the planks of the deck.

The sails of the ship bent in the wind and D'Averc cried out in astonishment. "That's what they're doing! They're driving the ship the way they want it to go! It's incredible!"

"We're heading back towards Amarehk," Hawkmoon said, struggling to rise. "I wonder . . ."

"What can their diet be?" D'Averc shouted. "Certainly they eat nothing intended to sweeten the breath! Phew!"

Hawkmoon grinned in spite of their plight.

The crew were now all huddled in the oar-wells, staring up fearfully at the monstrous reptiles as they flapped overhead, filling the sails with wind.

"Perhaps their nest is in this direction," Hawkmoon suggested. "Perhaps their young are to be fed and they prefer live meat?"

D'Averc looked offended. "What you say is likely, friend Hawkmoon. But it was still tactless of you to suggest it . . ."

Again Hawkmoon gave a wry grin.

"There's a chance, if their nests are on land, of getting to grips with them," he said. "On the open sea we had no chance of survival at all."

"You're optimistic, Duke of Köln . . ."

For more than an hour the extraordinary reptiles propelled the ship over the water at breakneck speed. Then at last Hawkmoon pointed ahead, saying nothing.

"An island!" exclaimed D'Averc. "You were right about that, at any rate!"

It was a small island, apparently bare of vegetation, its sides rising sharply to a peak, as if it was the tip of a drowned mountain that had not been entirely engulfed.

It was then that a fresh danger alerted Hawkmoon!

"Rocks! We're heading straight for them! Crew! To your positions. Helmsman . . ." But Hawkmoon was already dashing for the helm, had grabbed it and was desperately trying to save the ship from running on to the rocks.

D'Averc joined him, lending his own strength to turning the craft. The island loomed larger and larger and the sound of the surf boomed in their ears—a drumbeat of doom!

Slowly the ship turned as the cliffs of the island towered over them and the spray drenched them, but then they heard a terrible scraping sound which turned into a scream of tortured timbers and they knew that the rocks were ripping into the starboard side beneath the waterline.

"Every man for himself!" Hawkmoon cried and ran for the rail, D'Averc closely behind him. The ship lurched and reared like a living thing and all were flung back against the port rails of the craft. Bruised but still conscious, Hawkmoon and D'Averc pulled themselves to their feet, hesitated for a moment, then dived into the black and seething waters of the sea.

Weighted by his great broadsword, Hawkmoon felt himself being dragged to the bottom. Through the swirling water he saw other shapes drifting and the noise of the surf was now dull in his ears. But he would not release the Sword of the Dawn. Instead he fought to scabbard it and then use all his energy to strike up to the surface, dragging the heavy blade with him.

At last he broke through the waves and got a dim impression of the ship above him, but now the sea seemed much calmer and eventually the wind dropped altogether, the boom of the surf diminished to a whisper and a strange silence took the place of the cacophony of a few moments earlier. Hawkmoon headed for a flat rock, reached it, and dragged himself on to land.

Then he looked back.

The reptilian monsters were still wheeling in the sky, but so high up as not to disturb the air with their wing beats. Then they suddenly rose still higher into the sky, hovered for a moment, then dived headlong toward the sea.

One by one they struck the waves with a great smashing noise. The ship groaned as the wash hit it and Hawkmoon was almost sluiced from his place of safety.

Then the monsters were gone.

Hawkmoon wiped water from his eyes and spat out the brine from his mouth.

What would the monsters do next? Was it their intention to keep their prey alive, to pick them off when they needed fresh meat? There was no way of telling.

Hawkmoon heard a cry and saw D'Averc and half-a-dozen others come staggering along the rocks toward him.

D'Averc looked bewildered. "Did you see the beasts leave, Hawkmoon?"

"Aye. Will they be back, I wonder?"

D'Averc glanced grimly in the direction where the beasts had disappeared. He shrugged.

"I suggest we strike inland, saving what we can from the ship," Hawkmoon said. "How many of us left alive?" He turned enquiringly to the bosun who stood behind D'Averc.

"Most of us, I think, sir. We were lucky. Look." The bosun pointed beyond the ship to where the major part of the crew were assembling on the shore.

"Get some men back to the ship before she breaks up," Hawkmoon said. "Rig lines to the shore and start getting provisions to dry land."

"As you say, sir. But what if the monsters return?"

"We'll have to deal with them when we see them," Hawkmoon said.

For several hours Hawkmoon watched as everything possible was carried from the ship and piled on the rocks of the island.

"Can the ship be repaired, do you think?" D'Averc asked.

"Maybe. Now that the sea is calm, there's little chance of her breaking up. But it will take time." Hawkmoon fingered the dull, black stone in his forehead. "Come, D'Averc, let's explore inland."

They began to climb up over the rocks, heading up the

25

slope to the summit of the island. The place seemed completely devoid of life. The best they could hope to find would be pools of fresh water and there might be shellfish on the shore. It was a bleak place and their hopes of survival, if the ship could not be refloated, seemed very slight, particularly in view of the prospect of the monsters returning.

They reached the summit at last and paused, breathing heavily from their exertions.

"The other side's as barren as this," D'Averc said, gesturing downward. "I wonder . . ." He broke off and gasped. "By the Eyes of Berezenath! A man!"

Hawkmoon looked in the direction D'Averc indicated.

Sure enough, a figure was strolling along the shore below. As they stared, he looked up and waved cheerfully, gesturing them towards him.

Hardly sure if they were not suffering hallucinations, the two began slowly to climb down until they were close to the figure. He stood there, fists on his hips, feet wide apart, grinning at them. They paused.

The man was dressed in a peculiar and archaic fashion. Over his brawny torso was stretched a jerkin of leather, leaving his arms and chest bare. He wore a woollen bonnet on his mop of red hair and a pheasant's tail-feather was stuck jauntily into it. His breeks were of a strange chequered design and he wore battered buckled boots on his feet. Secured over his back by a cord was a gigantic battle-axe, its steel blade streaked with dirt and battered by much use. His face was bony and red and his pale blue eyes were sardonic as he stared at them.

"Well, now—you'd be the Hawkmoon and the D'Averc," he said in a strange accent. "I was told you'd likely come."

"And who are you, sir?" D'Averc asked somewhat haughtily.

"Why, I'm Orland Fank, didn't you know. Orland Fank —here at your service, good sirs."

"Do you live on this island?" Hawkmoon asked.

"I have lived on it, but not at the moment, don't you know." Fank removed his bonnet and wiped his forehead with his arm. "I'm a travelling man, these days. Like yourselves, I understand."

"And who told you of us?" Hawkmoon asked,

"I've a brother. Given to wearing somewhat fancy metal of black and gold . . ."

"The Warrior in Jet and Gold!" Hawkmoon exclaimed.

"He's called some such foppish title, I gather. He would not have mentioned his rough and ready brother to you, I don't doubt."

"He did not. Who are you?"

"I'm called Orland Fank. From Skare Brae—in the Orkneys, you know . . ."

"The Orkneys!" Hawkmoon's hand went to his sword. "Is that not part of Granbretan? Island to the far north!"

Fank laughed. "Tell an Orkney man that he belongs to the Dark Empire, and he'll tear the throat from you with his teeth!" He gestured apologetically, and as if in explanation said, "It's the favourite way of dealing with a foe out there, you know. We're not a sophisticated folk."

"So the Warrior in Jet and Gold is also from the Orkneys . . ." D'Averc began.

"Save you, no man! Him from the Orkneys, with his fancy suit of armour and his fine manner!" Orland Fank laughed heartily. "No. He's no Orkney man!" Fank wiped tears of laughter from his eyes with his battered bonnet. "Why should you think that?"

"You said he was your brother."

"So he is. Spiritually, you might say. Perhaps even physically. I've forgotten. It's been many years, you see, since we first came together."

"What brought you together?"

"A common cause, you might say. A shared ideal."

"And would the Runestaff be the source of that cause?" Hawkmoon murmured, his voice hardly louder than the whisper of the surf below them.

"It might."

"You seem close-mouthed, suddenly, friend Fank," said D'Averc.

"Aye. In Orkney, we're a close-mouthed folk," smiled Orland Fank. "Indeed, I'm considered something of a babbler there." He did not seem offended.

Hawkmoon gestured behind him. "Those monsters. The strange clouds we saw earlier. Would that be to do with the Runestaff?"

"I saw no monsters. No clouds. I've but recently arrived here myself."

"We were driven to this island by gigantic reptiles," Hawkmoon said. "And now I begin to see why. They, too, served the Runestaff, I do not doubt."

"That's as may be," Fank replied, "It's not my business, you see, Lord Dorian."

"Was it the Runestaff that caused our boat to be wrecked?" Hawkmoon asked fiercely.

"I could not say," Fank replied, replacing his bonnet on his mop of red hair and scratching at his bony chin. "I only know that I'm here to give you a boat and tell you where you might find the nearest habitable land."

"You have a boat for us?" D'Averc was astonished.

"Aye. Not a splendid one, but a seaworthy craft nonetheless. It should take the two of you."

"The two of us! We have a crew of fifty!" Hawkmoon's eyes blazed. "Oh, if the Runestaff wishes me to serve it, it should arrange things better! All it has succeeded in doing so far is to anger me fiercely!"

"Your anger will only weary you," Orland Fank replied mildly. "I had thought you bound for Dnark in the Runestaff's service. My brother told me . . ."

"Your brother insisted I go to Dnark. But I have other loyalties, Orland Fank—loyalties to the wife I have not seen for months, to the father-in-law who awaits my return, to my friends . . ."

"The folk of Castle Brass? Aye, I've heard of them. They are safe, for the moment, if that comforts you."

"You know this for certain?"

"Aye. Their lives are pretty much without event, save for the trouble with one Elvereza Tozer."

"Tozer! What of the renegade?"

"He secured back his ring, I gather, and left." Orland Fank made a flying gesture with his hand.

"For where?"

"Who knows? You have experience of the rings of Mygann yourself."

"They are untrustworthy objects."

"So I understand."

"They are well rid of Tozer, at any rate."

"I do not know the man."

"A talented playwright," Hawkmoon said, "with the moral rigour of a—of a . . ."

"A Granbretanian?" offered Fank.

"Exactly." Hawkmoon frowned then and stared hard at Orland Fank. "You would not deceive me? My kin and friends are safe?"

"Their security is not for the moment threatened."

Hawkmoon sighed. "Where is this boat? And what of my crew?"

"I have some small skill as a shipwright. I'll help them mend their ship so that they can return to Narleen."

"Why cannot we go with them?" D'Averc asked.

"I understood you were an impatient pair," Fank said innocently, "and that you would be off the island as soon as you could. It will take many days to repair the large craft."

"We'll take your little boat," Hawkmoon said. "It seems that if we did not, the Runestaff—or whatever power it was that really sent us here—would see to it that we were further inconvenienced."

"I understand that that would be likely," Fank agreed, smiling a little to himself.

"And how will you leave the island if we take your boat?" D'Averc asked.

"I'll sail with the seamen of Narleen. I have a great deal of time to spare."

"How far is it to the mainland?" Hawkmoon asked. "And by what shall we sail? Have you a compass to lend us?"

Fank shrugged. "It's of no great distance and you'll not need a compass. You need only wait for the right sort of wind."

"What do you mean?"

"The winds in these parts are somewhat peculiar. You will understand what I mean."

Hawkmoon shrugged in resignation.

They followed as Orland Fank led the way around the shore.

"It would seem that we are not quite as much the masters of our destinies as we should like," murmured D'Averc sardonically as the small boat came in sight.

29

CHAPTER FIVE

A CITY OF GLOWING SHADOWS

HAWKMOON LAY SCOWLING in the small boat and D'Averc whistled a tune as he stood in the prow, the spray lashing his face. For a whole day now the wind had guided the craft, blowing them on what was plainly a particular course.

"Now I understand what Fank meant about the wind," growled Hawkmoon. "This is no natural breeze. I resent the feeling of being some supernatural agency's puppet . . ."

D'Averc grinned and pointed ahead. "Well, perhaps we'll have a chance to voice our complaints to the agency itself. See—land in sight."

Hawkmoon rose reluctantly and saw the faint signs of land on the horizon.

"And so we return to Amarehk," laughed D'Averc.

"If only it were Europe and Yisselda were there," sighed Hawkmoon.

"Or even Londra, and Flana to comfort me." D'Averc shrugged and began to cough theatrically. "Still, it is best this way, lest she find herself pledged to a sick and dying creature . . ."

Gradually they could begin to make out features of the shoreline, of irregular cliffs, hills and beaches and some trees. Then, to their south, they saw a peculiar aura of golden light—light that seemed to throb as if in rhythm with a gigantic heart.

"More disturbing phenomena, it seems," said D'Averc.

The wind blew harder and the little boat turned toward the golden light.

"And we're heading directly for it," groaned Hawkmoon. "I am becoming tired of such things!"

Now it became clear that they were sailing into a bay formed by the mainland and a long island jutting out between the two shores and it was from the far end of this island that the golden light was pulsing.

The land on either side seemed pleasant, consisting of beaches and wooded hills, though there were no signs of habitation.

As they neared the source of the light, it began to fade until only a faint glow filled the sky and the boat's speed diminished, though they still sailed directly towards the light. Then they saw it.

It was a city of such grace and beauty that it robbed them of speech. As huge as Londra, if not larger, its buildings were symmetrical spires and domes and turrets, all glowing with the same strange light, but coloured in delicate, pale shades that lurked behind the gold—pink, yellow, blue, green, violet and cerise—like a painting that had been created in light and then washed with gold. And yet, for all its magnificent beauty, it did not seem somehow a habitation for human creatures, but for gods.

Now the ship was sailing into a harbour that stretched out from the city, its quays shifting with the same subtle shades they could see in the buildings.

"It is like a dream . . ." Hawkmoon murmured.

"A dream of heaven," answered D'Averc, his cynicism gone—vanished before the vision.

The little boat drifted to a set of steps that led down to the water, which was dappled with the reflections of the colours, and came to a halt.

D'Averc shrugged. "I suppose this is where we disembark. The boat could have borne us to a less pleasant place."

Hawkmoon nodded gravely and then said: "Are the Rings of Myggan still in your pouch, D'Averc?"

D'Averc patted his pouch. "They are safe. Why?"

"I wanted to know that if the danger was too great for us to face with our swords and there was time to use the rings, we could use them."

D'Averc nodded his understanding and then his forehead creased. "Strange that we did not think of using them on the island . . ."

Hawkmoon's face showed his astonishment. "Aye—aye . . ." And then he pursed his lips in disgust. "Doubtless that was the result of supernatural interference with our brains! How I hate the supernatural!"

D'Averc merrily put his fingers to his lips and put on an expression of mock disapproval. "What a thing to say in a city such as this!"

"Aye—well, I hope its inhabitants are as pleasant as its appearance."

"If it has any inhabitants," replied D'Averc glancing around him.

Together they climbed the steps and reached the quayside. The strange buildings were ahead of them and between the buildings ran wide streets.

"Let's enter the city," Hawkmoon said resolutely, "and find out why we have been taken here as soon as we can. Then, perhaps, we shall be allowed to return to Castle Brass!"

Entering the nearest street, it seemed to them that the shadows cast by the buildings actually glowed with a life and a colour of their own. At close hand the tall towers seemed hardly tangible and when Hawkmoon reached out to touch one the substance of it was unlike anything he had touched before. It was not stone and it was not timber; not steel even, for it gave slightly under his fingers and made them tingle. He was also surprised by the warmth that ran through his arm and suffused his body.

He shook his head. "It is more like flesh than stone!"

D'Averc reached out now and was equally astonished. "Aye — or like vegetation of some kind. It definitely seems organic — living stuff!"

They moved on. Every so often the long streets would broaden out into squares. They crossed the squares, choosing another street at random, looking up at the building which seemed of infinite height, which disappeared into the strange, golden haze.

Their voices were hushed, as if they hesitated to break the silence of the great city.

"Have you noticed," murmured Hawkmoon, "that there are no windows?"

"And no doors," nodded D'Averc. "I am certain that this city was not built for human use — and that humans did not build it!"

"Perhaps some beings created in the Tragic Millennium," Hawkmoon suggested. "Beings like the Wraith Folk of Soryandum."

D'Averc nodded his head in agreement.

Now ahead of them the strange shadows seemed to gather closer together and they passed into them, an impression of great well-being overcoming them. Hawkmoon began to smile in spite of his fears, and D'Averc, too, answered his smile. The glowing shadows swam around them. Hawkmoon began to wonder if perhaps these shadows were, in fact, the inhabitants of the city.

They passed out of the street and stood in a huge square that was without doubt the very centre of the city and there rising from the middle of the square was a cylindrical building that in spite of being the largest building in the city also seemed the most delicate. Its walls moved with colourful light and now Hawkmoon noticed something else at its base.

"Look, D'Averc — steps leading to a door!"

"What should we do, I wonder," whispered D'Averc.

Hawkmoon shrugged. "Enter, of course. What have we to lose?"

"Perhaps we shall discover the answer to that question within," smiled his friend. "After you, Duke of Köln!"

The two mounted the steps and climbed upward until they reached the doorway. It was relatively small — of human size in fact and within it they could see more of the glowing shadows.

Hawkmoon stepped bravely in with D'Averc immediately behind him.

CHAPTER SIX

JEHAMIA COHNAHLIAS

THEIR FEET SEEMED to sink into the floor and the glowing shadows seemed to wrap themselves around the two men as they advanced into the scintillating darkness of the tower.

A sweet sound now filled the corridors—a gentle sound like an unearthly lullaby. The music increased their sense of well-being as they pressed deeper into the strangely organic construction.

And then suddenly they stood in a small room, full of the same golden, pulsing radiance they had seen earlier from the boat.

And the radiance came from a child.

He was a boy, of oriental appearance, with a soft, brown skin, clad in robes on to which jewels had been stitched so that the fabric was completely hidden.

He smiled and his smile matched the gentle radiance surrounding him. It was impossible not to love him.

"Duke Dorian Hawkmoon von Köln," he said sweetly, bowing his head, "and Huillam D'Averc. I have admired both your painting and your buildings, sir."

D'Averc was astonished. "You know of those?"

"They are excellent. Why do you not do more?"

D'Averc coughed in embarrassment. "I—I lost the knack, I suppose. And then the war . . ."

"Ah, of course. The Dark Empire. That is why you are here."

"I would gather so—"

"I am called Jehamia Cohnahlias." The boy smiled again. "And that is the only direct information about myself I can offer you, in case you were going to ask me anything further. This city is called Dnark and its inhabitants are called in the outer world The Great Good Ones. You have encountered some of them already, I believe."

"The glowing shadows?" Hawkmoon asked.

"Is that how you perceive them? Yes—the glowing shadows."

"Are they sentient?" Hawkmoon queried.

"They are indeed. More than sentient, perhaps."

"And this city, Dnark," Hawkmoon said. "It is the legendary City of the Runestaff."

"It is."

"Strange that all those legends should place its position not on the continent of Amarehk, but in Asiacommunista, said D'Averc.

"Perhaps it is not a coincidence," smiled the boy. "It is convenient to have such legends."

"I understand."

Jehamia Cohnahlias smiled quietly.

"You have come to see the Runestaff, I gather?"

"Apparently," said Hawkmoon, unable to feel anger in the presence of the child. "First the Warrior in Jet and Gold told us to come here and then when we demurred we were introduced to his brother—one Orland Fank . . ."

"Ah, yes," smiled Jehamia Cohnahlias. "Orland Fank. I have a special affection for that particular servant of the Runestaff. Well, let us go to the Hall of the Runestaff." Then he frowned slightly. "But I was almost forgetting. First you will want to refresh yourselves and meet a fellow traveller. One who preceded you here by only a matter of hours."

"Do we know him?"

"I believe you have had some contact in the past."

The boy seemed almost to float down from his chair. "This way."

"Who can it be?" murmured D'Averc to Hawkmoon. "Who would we know who would come to Dnark?"

CHAPTER SEVEN

A WELL-KNOWN TRAVELLER

THEY FOLLOWED JEHEMIA Cohnahlias through the winding, organic corridors of the building. Now they were lighter, for the glowing shadows—the Great Good Ones as the boy had described them—had vanished. Presumably their task had been to help guide Hawkmoon and D'Averc to the child.

At last they entered a larger hall in which had been set a long table, presumably made of the same substance as the walls, and benches, also of the same stuff. Food had been laid on the table—relatively simple fare such as fish, bread and green vegetables.

But it was the figure at the far end of the hall who attracted their attention, that made their hands go automatically to their swords and their faces assume expressions of angry astonishment.

It was Hawkmoon who got the words out at last, between clenched teeth.

"Shenegar Trott!"

The fat figure moved heavily towards them, his plain, silver mask apparently a parody of the features beneath it.

"Good afternoon, gentlemen. Dorian Hawkmoon and Huillam D'Averc, I gather."

Hawkmoon turned to the boy. "Do you realise who this creature is?"

"An explorer from Europe, I gathered."

"He is the Count of Sussex—one of King Huon's right-hand men. He has raped half Europe! He is second only to Baron Meliadus in the evil he has wrought!"

"Come now," Trott said, his voice soft and amused. "Let us not begin by insulting each other. We are on neutral ground here. The issues of war are another matter. Since they do not at the moment concern us, then I suggest we behave in a civilised manner—and not insult our young host here . . ."

Hawkmoon glowered. "How did you come to Dnark, Count Shenegar?"

"By ship, Duke of Köln. Our Baron Kalan—whom I understand you have met . . ." Trott chuckled as Hawkmoon automatically put his hand to the black jewel Kalan had earlier placed there . . . "he invented a new kind of engine to propel our ships at great speed over the sea. Based on the engine that gives power to our ornithopters, I gather, but more sophisticated. I was commissioned by our wise King Emperor to journey to Amarahk, there to make friendly advances to the powers that dwelt here . . ."

"To discover their strengths and weaknesses before you attacked, you mean!" Hawkmoon shouted. "It is impossible to trust a servant of the Dark Empire!"

The boy spread his hands and a look of sorrow crossed his face. "Here in Dnark we seek only equilibrium. That, after all, is the goal and reason for existence of the Runestaff, which we are here to protect. Save your disputes, I beg you, for the battlefield and join together to eat the food we have prepared."

"But I must warn you," Huillam D'Averc said in a lighter tone than Hawkmoon had used, "that Shenegar Trott is not here to bring peace. Wherever he goes, he brings evil and disruption. Be prepared—for he is considered to be the most cunning lord in Granbretan."

The boy seemed embarrassed and merely gestured again to the table. "Please be seated."

"And where is your fleet, Count Shenegar?" D'Averc asked as he sat down on the bench and pulled a plate of fish towards him.

"Fleet?" Trott replied innocently. "I did not mention a fleet—only my ship, which is moored with its crew a few miles away from the city."

"Then it must be a large ship indeed," murmured Hawkmoon, biting at a hunk of bread, "for it is unlike a count of the Dark Empire to make a journey unprepared for conquest."

"You forget that we are scientists and scholars, too, in Granbretan," Trott said, as if mildly offended. "We seek knowledge and truth and reason. Why, our whole intention in uniting the warring states of Europe was to bring a rational peace to the world, so that knowledge might progress the faster."

D'Averc coughed theatrically, but said nothing.

Trott now did something that in a Dark Empire noble was virtually unprecedented, for he cheerfully pushed back his mask and began to eat. In Granbretan it was considered gross indecency both to display the face and to eat in public. Trott, Hawkmoon knew, had always been thought eccentric in Granbretan, tolerated by the other nobles only by virtue of his vast private fortune, his skill as a general and, in spite of his flabby appearance, a warrior of considerable personal courage.

The face revealed was plainly the one caricatured on the mask. It was white, plump and intelligent. The eyes were without expression, but it was plain Shenegar Trott could put whatever expression he chose into them.

They ate in relative silence. Only the boy touched none of the food, though he sat with them.

At length Hawkmoon gestured to the count's bulky silver armour. "Why do you travel in such heavy accoutrement, Count Shenegar, if you are on a peaceful mission of exploration?"

Shenegar Trott smiled. "Why—how was I to anticipate what dangers I should have to face in this strange city? Surely it is logical to travel well-prepared?"

D'Averc changed the subject as if he realised they would receive nothing but smooth answers from the Granbretanian. "How goes the war in Europe?" he asked.

"There is no war in Europe," Trott answered.

"No war! Then why should we be here—exiles from our own lands?" Hawkmoon said.

"There is no war, because all of Europe is now at peace under the patronage of our good King Huon," Shenegar Trott said, and then he gave a faint wink—almost a comradely wink—which made it impossible for Hawkmoon to reply.

"Save for the Kamarg, that is," Trott continued. "And that, of course, has vanished altogether. My fellow peer Baron Meliadus was quite enraged by that."

"I'm sure he was," said Hawkmoon. "And does he still continue his vendetta against us?"

Indeed he does. In fact when I left Londra, he was in danger of becoming a laughing stock at court."

"You seem to feel little affection for Baron Meliadus," D'Averc suggested.

"You understand me well," Count Shenegar told him. "You see we are not all such insane and greedy men as you would think. I have many disputes with Baron Meliadus. Though I am loyal to my motherland and my leader, I do not agree with everything done in their names —indeed, what I myself have done. I follow my orders. I am a patriot." Shenegar Trott shrugged his bulky shoulders. "I would prefer to stay at home, reading and writing. I was once thought a promising poet, you know."

"But now you write only epitaphs—and those in blood and fire," Hawkmoon said.

Count Shenegar did not seem hurt. Instead he replied reasonably. "You have your point of view, I have mine. I believe in the ultimate sanity of our cause—that the unification of the world is of maximum importance, that personal ambitions, no matter how noble, must be sacrificed to the larger principles."

"That is the usual bland Granbretanian answer," Hawkmoon said, unconvinced. "It is the argument that Meliadus used to Count Brass shortly before he attempted to rape and carry off his daughter Yisselda!"

"I have already disassociated myself from Baron Meliadus," Count Shenegar said. "Every court must have its fool, every great ideal must attract some who are motivated only by self-interest."

Shenegar Trott's answers seemed more directed at the quietly listening boy than at Hawkmoon and D'Averc themselves.

The meal finished, Trott pushed back his plate and resettled his silver mask over his face. He turned to the boy. "I thank you, sir, for your hospitality. Now—you promised me I might look upon and admire the Runestaff. It will give me great joy to stand before that legendary artefact . . ."

Hawkmoon and D'Averc glanced warningly at the boy, but he did not appear to notice.

"It is late, now," said Jehemia Cohnahlias. "We shall all visit the Hall of the Runestaff tomorrow. Meanwhile rest here. Through that little door," he gestured across the room, "you will find sleeping accommodation. I will call for you in the morning."

Shenegar Trott rose and bowed. "I thank you for your offer, but my men will become agitated if I do not return to my ship tonight. I will rejoin you here tomorrow."

"As you wish," the boy said.

"We would be grateful to you for your hospitality," Hawkmoon said. "But again let us warn you that Shenegar Trott may not be what he would have you believe."

"You are admirable in your tenacity," Shenegar Trott said. He waved a gauntletted hand in a cheerful salute and strode jauntily from the hall.

"I fear we shall sleep poorly knowing that our enemy is in Dnark," said D'Averc.

The boy smiled. "Fear not. The Great Good Ones will help you rest and protect you from any harm you may fear. Goodnight, gentlemen. I shall see you tomorrow."

The boy walked lightly from the room and D'Averc and Hawkmoon went to inspect the cubicles containing bunks and bedding that were let into the side of the walls.

"I fear that Shenegar Trott means the boy harm," Hawkmoon said.

"We had best make it our business to protect him, if we can," D'Averc replied. "Goodnight, Hawkmoon."

After D'Averc had ducked into his cubicle, Hawkmoon entered his own. It was full of glowing shadows and the soft music of the unearthly lullaby he had heard earlier. Almost immediately he was sound asleep.

CHAPTER EIGHT

AN ULTIMATUM

HAWKMOON AWOKE LATE feeling thoroughly rested, but then he noticed that the glowing shadows seemed agitated. They had turned to a cold, blue colour and were swirling around as if in fear!

Hawkmoon rose quickly and buckled on his sword belt. He frowned. Was the danger he had feared about to come —or had it come already? The Great Good Ones seemed incapable of human communication.

D'Averc came running into Hawkmoon's cubicle.

"What do you think is the matter, Hawkmoon?"

"I do not know. Is Shenegar Trott scheming some invasion? Is the boy in trouble?"

But then suddenly the glowing shadows had wrapped themselves chillingly around the two men and they felt themselves whisked from the cubicle, through the room in which they had eaten, and along the corridors at incredible speed until they broke out of the building altogether and were whirled upward into the golden light.

Now the speed of the Great Good Ones decreased and Hawkmoon and D'Averc, still breathless at the sudden action of the glowing shadows, hovered in the air high above the main square.

D'Averc looked pale, for his feet were planted on nothing and the glowing shadows seemed to have even less substance, yet they did not fall.

Down in the square tiny figures could be seen moving in towards the cylindrical tower.

"It is an entire army!" Hawkmoon gasped. "There must be at least a thousand of them. So much for Shenegar Trott's claims for the peaceful nature of his mission. He has invaded Dnark! But why?"

"Isn't it obvious to you, my friend," said D'Averc grimly. "He seeks the Runestaff itself. With that in his power, he would doubtless rule the world!"

"But he does not know its location!"

"That is probably why he is attacking the tower. See—there are warriors already inside!"

Surrounded by the flimsy shadows, and with golden light on all sides, the two men looked at the scene in dismay.

"We must descend," Hawkmoon said finally.

"But we are only two against a thousand!" D'Averc pointed out.

"Aye—but if the Sword of the Dawn will again summon the Legion of the Dawn, then we might succeed against them!" Hawkmoon reminded him.

As if they had understood his words, the Great Good Ones began to descend. Hawkmoon felt his heart enter his throat as they dropped rapidly towards the square, now thickly clustered with masked Dark Empire warriors —members of the terrible Falcon Legion which, like the Vulture Legion, was a mercenary force made up of renegades who were, if anything, more evil than the native Granbretanians. The mad Falcon eyes stared up as if in anticipation of the feast of blood that Hawkmoon and D'Averc offered, the beaks seemed ready to tear the flesh of the two enemies of the Dark Empire, and the swords, maces, axes and spear in their hands seemed like talons ready to rend.

The glowing shadows deposited D'Averc and the Duke of Köln near the entrance to the tower and they just had time to draw their blades before the Falcons attacked.

But then Shenegar Trott appeared at the entrance of the tower and called to his men.

"Stop, my falcons. There is no need for bloodshed. I have the boy!"

Hawkmoon and D'Averc saw him lift the child, Jehemia Cohnahlias, by his robes and hold him struggling before them.

"I know that this city is full of supernatural creatures who would seek to stop us," the Count announced, "and thus I have taken the liberty of insuring our safety while we are here. If we are attacked. If one of us is touched, I shall slit the little boy's throat from ear to ear." Shenegar Trott chuckled. "I take this step only to avoid unpleasantness on all sides . . ."

42

Hawkmoon made to move, to summon the Legion of the Dawn, but Trott wagged his finger chidingly. "Would you be the cause of a child's death, Duke of Köln?"

Glowering, Hawkmoon dropped his swordarm, addressing the boy. "I warned you of his perfidy!"

"Aye . . ." the boy struggled, half-choking in his robes. "I fear I should have—paid more—attention to you, sir."

Count Shenegar laughed, his mask flashing in the golden light. "Now—tell me where the Runestaff is kept."

The boy pointed back into the tower. "The Hall of the Runestaff is within."

"Show me!" Shenegar Trott turned to his men. "Watch this pair. I'd rather have them alive, since the King Emperor will be well-pleased if we can return with both the Heroes of Kamarg and the Runestaff. If they move, shout to me and I'll take off an ear or two." He drew his dirk and held it near the boy's face. "Most of you—follow me."

Shenegar Trott disappeared once more into the tower and six of the Falcon warriors stayed to guard Hawkmoon and D'Averc while the rest followed their leader.

Hawkmoon scowled. "If only the boy had paid heed to what we said!" He moved slightly and the Falcons stirred warningly. "Now how are we to save him—and the Runestaff—from Trott?"

Suddenly the Falcons looked upward in astonishment and D'Averc's gaze followed theirs.

"It seems we are to be rescued," smiled D'Averc.

The glowing shadows were returning.

Before the Falcons could move or speak, the shadows had wrapped themselves around the two men and were once again lifting them upwards.

Disconcerted, the Falcons slashed at their feet as they ascended, and then turned to run into the tower, to warn their leader of what had happened.

Higher and higher rose the Great Good Ones, carrying Hawkmoon and D'Averc with them. Into the golden haze that became a thick, golden mist so that they could no longer see each other, let alone the buildings of the city.

They seemed to travel for hours before they became aware of the golden mist thinning.

CHAPTER NINE

THE RUNESTAFF

As the golden mist diminished, Hawkmoon blinked his eyes, for they were now assailed by all manner of colours—waves and rays making strange configurations in the air—and all emanating from a central source.

Narrowing his eyes against the light, he peered around him. They hovered near the roof of a hall whose walls seemed constructed of sheets of translucent emerald and onyx. At the centre of the hall rose a dais, reached by steps from all sides. It was from the object on this dais that the configurations of light originated. The patterns—stars, circles, cones and more complex figures—shifted constantly, but their source was always the same. It was a small staff, about the length of a short sword, of a dense black, dull and apparently discoloured in a few places. The discolorations were of a deep, mottled blue.

Could this be the Runestaff? Hawkmoon wondered. It seemed unimpressive for an object of such legendary powers. He had imagined it taller than a man, of brilliant colours—but that thing he could carry in one hand!

Suddenly, from the side of the hall, men thrust themselves in. It was Shenegar Trott and his Falcon Legion. The little boy still struggled in Trott's grasp and now the laughter of the Count of Sussex began to fill the hall.

"At last! And it is mine! Even the King Emperor will not dare to deny me anything once the Runestaff itself is in my hands."

Hawkmoon sniffed. There was a fragrant, bitter-sweet smell in the air. And now a mellow humming sound began to fill the hall. The Great Good Ones began to lower himself and D'Averc until they stood high on the steps, just below the Runestaff. And then Count Shenegar saw them.

"How . . .?"

Hawkmoon glared down at him, raised his left arm to

point directly at him. "Release the child, Shenegar Trott!"

The Count of Sussex chuckled again, recovering quickly from his astonishment. "First tell me how you arrived here before me."

"By means of the help of the Great Good Ones—those supernatural creatures you feared. And we have other friends, Count Shenegar."

Trott's dirk leapt to within a hairsbreadth of the boy's nose. "I would be a fool, then, to release my only chance of freedom—not to say success!"

Hawkmoon lifted up the Sword of the Dawn. I warn you, count, this blade I bear is no ordinary instrument! See how it glows with rosy light!"

"Aye—it is very pretty. But can it stop me before I pluck one of the boy's eyes from his skull, like a plum from the jar?"

D'Averc glanced about the strange room, at the constantly changing patterns of light, at the peculiar walls, and the glowing shadows now high above which seemed to be looking on. "It seems to be stalemate, Hawkmoon," he murmured. "We can get no further help from the glowing shadows, by the look of it. Evidently they are powerless to take a part in human affairs."

"If you'd release the boy, I'd consider letting you leave Dnark unharmed," Hawkmoon said.

Shenegar Trott laughed. "Indeed? And you would chase an army from the city, you two?"

"We are not without allies," Hawkmoon reminded him.

"Possibly. But I suggest you lay down your own swords and let me up to the Runestaff there. When I have that, you may have the boy."

"Alive?"

"Alive."

"How can we trust Shenegar Trott of all men?" D'Averc said. "He will kill the boy and then dispose of us. It is not the way of the nobles of Granbretan to keep their words."

"If only we had some guarantee," whispered Hawkmoon desperately.

At that moment a familiar voice spoke from behind them and they turned in surprise.

"You have no choice but to release the child, Shenegar

Trott!" The voice boomed from within a helm of jet and gold.

"Aye, my brother speaks the truth . . ." From the other side of the dais Orland Fank now emerged, his gigantic war-axe on his leather-clad shoulder.

"How did you get here?" Hawkmoon asked in astonishment.

"I might ask the same," grinned Fank. "At least you now have friends with whom to debate this dilemma."

CHAPTER TEN

SPIRIT OF THE RUNESTAFF

SHENEGAR TROTT, COUNT of Sussex, chuckled again and shook his head. "Well, there are now four of you, but it does not alter the situation a scrap. I have a thousand men at my back. I have the boy. You will kindly step aside, gentlemen, while I take the Runestaff for my own."

Orland Fank's rawboned face split in a huge grin, while the Warrior in Jet and Gold merely shifted his armoured feet a little. Hawkmoon and D'Averc look questioningly at them. "I think there is a weakness in your argument, my friend," said Orland Fank.

"Oh, no, sir—there is none." Shenegar Trott began to move forward.

"Aye—I'd say that there was."

Trott paused. "What is it, then?"

"You are assuming you can hold yon boy, are you not?"

"I could kill him before you could take him."

"Aye—but you're assuming the child has no means of escaping from you, are you not?"

"He can't wriggle free!" Shenegar Trott held the child up by the slack of his garments and began to laugh loudly. "See!"

And then the Granbretanian yelled in astonishment as the boy seemed to flow from his grasp, streaking out across the hall in a long strip of light, his features still visible but oddly elongated. The music swelled in the hall and the odour increased.

Shenegar Trott made ineffectual grabbing motions at the boy's thinning substance but it was as impossible to grasp him as it was to grasp the glowing shadows that now pulsed in the air above them.

"By Huon's Globe—he is not human!" screamed Trott in frustrated anger. "He is *not* human!"

"He did not claim to be," Orland Fank said mildly and

winked cheerfully at Hawkmoon. "Are you and your friend ready for a good fight, now?"

"We are," grinned Hawkmoon. "We are indeed!"

Now the boy—or whatever it was—was stretching out over their heads to touch the Runestaff. The configurations changed rapidly and many more of them now filled the hall so that all their faces were crossed with shifting bars of colour.

Orland Fank watched this with great attention and it seemed that as the boy was actually absorbed into the Runestaff the Orkneyman's face saddened as if in regret.

Soon there was no trace of the boy in the hall and the Runestaff now glowed a brighter black, seemed to have assumed sentience.

Hawkmoon gasped. "Who was he, Orland Fank?"

Fank blinked. "Who? Why, the spirit of the Runestaff. He rarely materialises in human form. You were especially honoured."

Shenegar Trott was screaming in fury but then broke off as a great voice boomed from the closed helm of the Warrior in Jet and Gold. "Now you must prepare yourself for death, Count of Sussex."

Trott laughed crazily. "You are still mistaken. There are four of you—a thousand of us. You shall die, and then I shall claim the Runestaff!"

The Warrior turned to Hawkmoon. "Duke of Köln, would you care to summon some aid?"

"With pleasure," grinned Hawkmoon and he raised the rosy sword high in the air. *"I summon the Legion of the Dawn!"*

And then a rosy light filled the hall, flooding over the colourful patterns in the air. And there stood a hundred fierce warriors, framed each in his own scarlet aura.

The warriors had a barbaric appearance, as if they came from an earlier, more primitive age. They bore great spiked clubs decorated with ornate carvings, lances bound with tufts of dyed hair. Their brown bodies and faces were smeared with paint and clad in loincloths of bright cloth. On their arms and legs were strapped wooden plates for protection. Their large black eyes were full of a remote sorrow and they gave voice to a mournful, moaning dirge.

These were the Warriors of the Dawn.

Even the hardened members of the Falcon Legion cried out in horror as the warriors appeared from nowhere. Shenegar Trott took a step backward.

"I would advise you to lay down your weapons and make yourselves our prisoners," Hawkmoon advised grimly.

Trott shook his head. "Never. There are still more of us than there are of you!"

"Then we must begin our battle," Hawkmoon said, and he began to move down the steps towards his enemies.

Now Shenegar Trott drew his own great battleblade and dropped to a fighting position. Hawkmoon swung at him with the Sword of the Dawn, but Trott dodged aside, swinging at Hawkmoon and barely missing gouging a line across his stomach. Hawkmoon was at a disadvantage, for Trott was fully armoured, while Hawkmoon wore only silk.

The dirge of the Soldiers of the Dawn changed to a great howl as they rushed down the steps behind Hawkmoon and began to hack and stab about them with clubs and lances. The fierce Falcon fighters met them valiantly, giving as good as they received, but were plainly demoralised when they discovered that for every Warrior of the Dawn that they slew another appeared from nowhere to take his place.

D'Averc, Orland Fank and the Warrior in Jet and Gold moved more slowly down the steps, swinging their blades in unison before them and driving back the Falcons with three pendulums of steel.

Shenegar Trott struck again at Hawkmoon and ripped the sleeve of his shirt. Hawkmoon flung out his sword-arm and the Sword of the Dawn met Trott's mask, denting it so that the features took on an even more grotesque appearance.

But then, as Hawkmoon leapt backward, poised to continue the fight, he felt a sudden blow on the back of his head, half-turned and saw a Falcon warrior had struck him with the haft of an axe. He tried to recover, but then began to fall. As he lost his senses, he saw the Warriors of Dawn begin to fade into oblivion. Desperately he tried to recover, for the Warriors of Dawn, it seemed, could not exist unless he had control of his senses.

But it was too late. As he fell to the steps, he heard Shenegar Trott chuckling.

CHAPTER ELEVEN

A BROTHER SLAIN

HAWKMOON HEARD THE distant din of battle, shook his head and peered through a haze of red and black. He tried to rise, but realised that at least four corpses pinned him down. His friends had taken good account of themselves.

Struggling up, he saw that Shenegar Trott had reached the Runestaff. And there stood the Warrior in Jet and Gold, evidently badly wounded, hacked at by a hundred blades, attempting to stop the Granbretanian from reaching the Runestaff. But Shenegar Trott raised a huge mace and brought it down on the Warrior's helm. He staggered and the helm crumpled.

Hawkmoon gathered his breath to cry hoarsely: "Legion of the Dawn! Return to me! Legion of the Dawn!"

And then the barbaric warriors began to reappear, lashing about them at the startled Falcons.

Hawkmoon began to stagger up the steps to the Warrior's aid, unable to see if any of the others lived. But then the huge weight of the jet and gold armour began to fall towards him, knocking him backwards. He supported it as best he could, but he knew by the feel of it that there was no life left in the body within.

He forced back the visor, weeping for the man he had never considered a friend until now, curious to see the features of the one who had guided his destiny for so long, but the visor would hardly move an inch, for Shenegar Trott's mace had buckled it so.

"Warrior . . ."

"The warrior is dead!" Shenegar Trott had flung off his mask and was reaching for the Runestaff, triumphantly staring back over his shoulder at Hawkmoon. "As shall you be in a trice, Dorian Hawkmoon!"

With a shout of fury, Hawkmoon dropped the Warrior's corpse and flew up the steps towards his enemy. Disconcerted, Trott turned, raising the mace again.

Hawkmoon ducked the blow and closed with Trott, grappling with him on the topmost step while red carnage was spread all around them.

As he struggled with the count, he saw D'Averc, half-way up the steps, his shirt a mass of bloody rags, one arm limp at his side, tackling five of the Falcon warriors —and higher up Orland Fank was still alive, whirling his battle-axe around his head and giving voice to a strange, skirling cry.

Trott's breath wheezed from between his fat lips and Hawkmoon was astonished at his strength. "You will die, Hawkmoon—you must die if the Runestaff is to be mine! "

Hawkmoon panted as he wrestled with the count. "It will never be yours. It can be possessed by no man! "

With a sudden heave, he broke Trott's guard and punched him full in the face. The count screamed and came forward again, but Hawkmoon raised his booted foot and kicked him in the chest, sending him reeling back against the dais. Then Hawkmoon recovered his sword and when Shenegar Trott ran at him again, blind with anger, he ran directly on to the point of the Sword of the Dawn, dying with an obscene curse on his lips and one last, backward look at the Runestaff.

Hawkmoon tugged the sword free and looked about him. His Legion of the Dawn were finishing their work, clubbing down the last of the Falcons, and D'Averc and Fank were leaning exhaustedly against the dais beneath the Runestaff.

Soon a few groans were cut short as spiked clubs fell on heads, and then there was silence save for the faint, melodic humming and the heavy breathing of the three survivors.

As the last Granbretanian died, the Legion of the Dawn vanished.

Hawkmoon stared down at the fat corpse of Shenegar Trott and he frowned. "We have slain one—but if one has been sent here, then others will follow. Dnark is no longer safe from the Dark Empire."

Fank sniffed and wiped his nose with his forearm. "It is for you to make sure that Dnark is safe—that the rest of the world is safe, in fact."

Hawkmoon smiled sardonically. "And how may I do that?"

Fank began to speak and then his eyes lighted on the huge corpse of the Warrior in Jet and Gold and he gasped: "Brother!" and began to stagger down the steps, to drop his battle axe and gather the armoured figure in his arms. "Brother . . .?"

"He is dead," Hawkmoon said softly. "He died by Shenegar Trott's hand, defending the Runestaff. I slew Trott . . ."

Fank wept.

At length they stood together, the three of them, looking about at the carnage. The whole hall of the Runestaff was full of corpses. Even the patterns in the air seemed to have taken on a reddish colouring and the bitter-sweet odour could not disguise the stink of death.

Hawkmoon scabbarded the Sword of the Dawn. "What now, I wonder?" he said. "We've done the work we were asked to do. We've defended the Runestaff successfully. Now do we return to Europe."

Then a voice spoke from behind them; it was the sweet voice of the child, Jehemia Cohnahlias. Turning, Hawkmoon saw that he now stood beside the Runestaff, holding it in one hand.

"Now Duke of Köln you take what you have rightfully earned," said the boy, his slanting eyes full of warm humour. "You take the Runestaff with you back to Europe, there to decide the destiny of the Earth."

"To Europe! I thought it could not be removed from its place."

"Not by any man. You, as the chosen one of the Runestaff, may take it." The boy stretched out towards Hawkmoon, and in his hand was the Runestaff. "Take it. Defend it. And pray it defends you."

"And how shall we use it?" D'Averc enquired.

"As your standard. Let all men know that the Runestaff rides with you—that the Runestaff is on your side. Tell them that it was the Baron Meliadus who dared swear an oath on the Runestaff and thus set into motion these events which will destroy completely one protagonist or the other. Whatever happens, it will be final. Carry your invasion to Granbretan if you can, or else die in the effort. The last great battle between Meliadus and Hawkmoon is soon to be fought, and over it the Runestaff will preside!"

Hawkmoon mutely accepted the staff. It felt cold, dead and very heavy, though the patterns still blazed about it.

"Put it inside your shirt, or wrap it in a cloth," advised the boy, "and none will observe those betraying forces that surround the Runestaff until you should wish them revealed."

"Thank you," said Hawkmoon quietly.

"The Great Good Ones will help you return to your home," the boy continued. "Farewell, Hawkmoon."

"Farewell? Where do you go now?"

"Where I belong."

And suddenly the boy began to change again, turning into a streamer of golden light that still had some semblance of human shape, pouring itself into the Runestaff that immediately became warm, vital and light in Hawkmoon's grasp.

With a slight shudder, Hawkmoon tucked the Runestaff inside his shirt.

As they walked out of the hall, D'Averc observed that Orland Fank was still weeping softly.

"What disturbs you, Fank?" D'Averc asked. "Do you still grieve the man who was your brother."

"Aye—but I grieve my son the more."

"Your son? What of him?"

Orland Fank jerked his thumb at Hawkmoon, who wandered behind, his head bowed in thought. "He has him."

"What do you mean?"

Fank sighed. "It must be, I know that. But still, I am a man, I can weep. I speak of Jehemia Cohnahlias."

"The boy! The spirit of the Runestaff?"

"Aye. He was my son—or myself—I have never quite understood these things . . ."

BOOK TWO

CHAPTER ONE

WHISPERING IN SECRET ROOMS

As it is written: "Those who swear by the Rune-staff must then benefit or suffer from the conse-quences of the fixed pattern of destiny that they set in motion." And Baron Meliadus of Kroiden had sworn such an oath, had sworn vengeance against all of Castle Brass, had sworn that Yisselda, Count Brass's daughter, would be his. On that day, many months earlier, he had fixed the pat-tern of fate; a pattern that had involved him in strange, destructive schemes, that had involved Dorian Hawkmoon in wild and uncanny adven-tures in distant places, and that was now nearing its terrible resolution.
    —The High History of the Runestaff

THE VERANDAH OVERLOOKED the blood-red river Tayme that made its sluggish way through the very heart of Londra, between gloomy, crazy towers.

Above them the occasional ornithopter, a bright bird of metal, clanked past, and on the river the barges of bronze and ebony carried cargo to and from the coast. Those cargoes were rich; full of stolen goods and stolen men, women and children brought as slaves to Londra. An awning of heavy purple velvet hung with tassels of scarlet silk protected the occupants of the veranda from view from above and the awning's shadow made it im-possible for them to be seen from the river.

A table of brass and two golden chairs upholstered in blue plush stood on the verandah. A richly decorated platinum tray on the table bore a wine jug of dark green glass and two matching goblets. On either side of the door leading on to the verandah stood a naked girl, with face, breasts and genitals heavily rouged. Anyone familiar with the Court of Londra would have recognised the slave girls as belonging to Baron Meliadus of Kroiden, for he had only female slaves and their only livery was the rouge he insisted they wear. One of the girls, who stared fixedly out at the river, was a blonde, almost certainly from Köln in Germany, which was one of the baron's possessions by right of conquest. The other girl was dark, doubtless from some town in the Middle East that Baron Meliadus had added, by means of a bloodied sword, to his estates.

In one of the golden chairs sat a woman, clad from head to foot in rich brocade and wearing a silver mask, delicately fashioned to resemble a heron. In the other sat a figure dressed in bulky black leather, his shoulders crowned by a huge mask representing a black, snarling wolf. He inserted a golden tube into his goblet and stuck the other end through a tiny aperture in the mask, beginning to suck slowly at the wine.

There was silence between the pair and the only sound came from beyond the verandah—from the wake of the barges slapping at the wall, from a distant tower as someone screamed and laughed at once, from an ornithopter high above, its metal wings flapping slowly as it sought to land on the flat top of one of the towers.

And then, at length, the figure in the mask began to speak in a low, thrilling voice. The other figure did not move its head or appear to hear but continued to stare out over the blood red water whose strange colour was attributed to the effluvia which poured from outlets near its bed.

"You are under some slight suspicion yourself, you know, Flana. King Huon suspects that you might have had something to do with the mysterious madness that overwhelmed the guards the night the Asiacommunistans escaped. Doubtless I am not helping my own cause by seeing you thus, but I think only of our beloved homeland—only of the glory of Granbretan."

The speaker paused as if expecting a reply, but received none.

"It is plain, Flana, that the present situation of the

56

Court is not in the best interests of the Empire. I delight in eccentricity, of course, as a true son of Granbretan, but there is a difference between eccentricity and senility. You take my meaning?"

Flana Mikosevaar said nothing.

"I am suggesting," continued the other, "that we need a new ruler—an Empress. There is only one alive who is a direct blood relative of Huon—only one that all will accept as a rightful liege, a rightful inheritor to the throne of the Dark Empire."

Again no reply.

The figure in the wolf mask bent forward. "Flana?"

The heron mask turned to regard the snarling wolf visage.

"Flana—you could be Queen-Empress of Granbretan. With myself as Regent, we could ensure the security of our nation and our territories, make Granbretan greater —make the whole world ours!"

"And what would be done with the world once we owned it, Meliadus?" For the first time Flana Mikosevaar spoke.

"Enjoy it, Flana! Use it!"

"Cannot one tire of rape and murder? Of torture and destruction?"

Meliadus seemed puzzled by her comment. "One can become bored by anything, of course, but there are other things—there are Kalan's experiments—and Taragorm's for that matter. With the resources of the world at their disposal, our scientists could make anything. Why, they could build us ships to sail through space, as the ancients had and as the one in which legend says The Runestaff was brought to our globe! We could journey to new worlds and conquer them—pitting wits and skill against a universe! Granbretan's adventure could last a million years!"

"And is adventure and sensation all we should seek, Meliadus?"

"Aye—why not? All is chaos, there is no meaning to existence, there is only one advantage to living one's life and that is to discover all the sensations that the human mind and body is capable of feeling. That will take at least a million years, surely?"

Flana nodded. "That is our creed, true." She appeared to sigh. "Therefore I suppose I can agree to your plans, Meliadus, for what you suggest I do is doubtless no more boring than anything else." She shrugged. "Very well, I will be your Queen when you need me—and if Huon discovers our perfidy, why, it will be a relief to die."

Slightly unnerved by this, Meliadus rose from the table. "You will say nothing to anyone until the time comes, Flana?"

"I will say nothing."

"Good. Now I must visit Kalan. He is attracted to my scheme, since it means more scope for his experiments if we succeed. Taragorm, too, is with me . . ."

"You trust Taragorm? Your rivalry is well-known."

"Aye— I hate Taragorm, it is true, and he hates me, but it is a mellow sort of hatred now, for you'll remember that our rivalry began over Taragorm's marriage to my sister whom I had previously intended to wed myself. But my sister compromised herself—with a jackass, I heard—and Taragorm discovered it. Whereupon, as you no doubt heard, my sister had her slaves slaughter her and the ass in some strange manner. Taragorm and I disposed of the slaves jointly and during that episode we rediscovered something of our old comradeship. My brother-in-law may be trusted. He feels Huon hampers his researches too much."

All this time their voices had not risen above a murmur so that even the slavegirls by the door could not hear them.

Now Meliadus bowed to Flana, snapped his fingers at the girls so that they ran to prepare his litter and carry him back through the corridors to his own home, and left.

Flana continued to stare out over the water, hardly thinking of Meliadus's scheme, but dreaming instead of the handsome D'Averc and of days in the future when they might meet again and D'Averc would take her away from Londra and all its intrigues—take her perhaps to his own rural estates in France which she, if she were Queen, would be able to give back to him.

Perhaps there would be an advantage to her becoming Queen Empress, then? That way she could choose her husband and that husband would be, of course, D'Averc. She could pardon him for his crimes against Granbretan, perhaps even pardon his companions—Hawkmoon and the rest.

But no, Meliadus might agree to D'Averc's reprieve—he would not agree to sparing all the rest.

Perhaps her scheme was foolish. She sighed. She did not altogether care. There was even doubt that D'Averc was still alive. In the meantime she saw no reason for not taking at least a passive part in Meliadus's treason, although even she had some inkling of the awful consequences of failure, of the magnitude of Meliadus's scheme. He must be desperate indeed to consider overthrowing his hereditary ruler. In all the two thousand years of his rule, no Granbretanian had previously dared think of deposing Huon. Flana did not even know if it were possible.

She shuddered. If she became Queen, she would not choose immortality—particularly if it meant becoming a wizened thing like Huon.

CHAPTER TWO

CONVERSATION BESIDE THE MENTALITY MACHINE

KALAN OF VITALL fingered his serpent mask with pale, old hands on which the veins stood out, resembling, themselves, so many curling blue snakes. Before them was the main laboratory—a great, low-ceilinged hall in which many experiments were being performed by men dressed in the uniforms and masks of the Order of the Serpent, of which Baron Kalan was Grand Constable. Strange machines gave off stranger sounds and stenches and miniature coloured lightnings flashed and cracked around them so that the entire area resembled some hellish workshop presided over by devils. Here and there human beings of both sexes and varying ages had been strapped out or fitted into machines as the scientists tested their experiments on the human mind and body. Most had been silenced in some way, but a few screamed or moaned or cried out in peculiar insane voices, often to the annoyance of the distracted scientists who would stuff rags into the mouths or sever vocal chords or find some other swift method of achieving a measure of quiet while they worked.

Kalan put one hand on Meliadus's shoulder and pointed to a machine that stood unattended nearby.

"You'll remember the mentality machine? The one we used to test Hawkmoon's mind?"

"Aye," Meliadus grumbled. "That's the one that led you to believe that we could trust Hawkmoon."

"We reckoned without factors we could not anticipate," Kalan said by way of defence. "Well, that is not why I mentioned my little invention. I was asked to use it this morning."

"By whom?"

"By the King Emperor himself. He summoned me to the Throne Room and told me he wished to test a member of the Court."

60

"Who?"

"Who d'you think, my lord?"

"Myself!" Meliadus spoke with outrage.

"Exactly. I think he suspects your loyalty in some way, lord baron . . ."

"How much, do you think?"

"Not much. All that appears to be in Huon's mind is that you may be concentrating too much on your personal schemes and not enough on the interests of his own plans. I think he would merely like to know how strong your loyalty is and if you have given up your personal plans . . ."

"Do you intend to obey his orders, Kalan?"

Kalan shrugged. "Do you suggest I ignore them?"

"No—but what shall we do?"

"I will have to put you in the mentality machine, of course, but I think I can obtain the results that would be most in our interest." Kalan chuckled, a hollow whisper of sound from within his mask. "Shall we begin, Meliadus?"

Meliadus moved reluctantly forward, looking nervously at the gleaming machine of red and blue metal, with its mysterious projections, its heavy, jointed arms and attachments of unknown application. Its main feature, however, was the huge bell that hung above the rest of the machine, depending from an intricate scaffold.

Now Kalan threw a switch and gestured apologetically. "We once kept this machine in a hall of its own, but space has become so limited of late. That is one of my chief complaints. We are asked for so much and given so little space in which to achieve it." Now from the machine came a sound like the breathing of some gigantic beast. Meliadus took a step backward. Kalan chuckled again and signalled for serpent-masked servitors to come to help him operate the mentality machine.

"If you will kindly stand beneath the bell, Meliadus, we will lower it at once," Kalan suggested.

Slowly, suspiciously, Meliadus took his place beneath the bell as it began to descend until it had completely covered him, its fleshy sides writhing until they had moulded themselves completely to his body. Then Meliadus felt as if hot wires had been inserted into his skull and that they were probing in his brain. He tried to yell, but was muffled. Hallucinations began—visions and memories of his past life—mainly of battles and bloodshed, though the hated face of Dorian Hawkmoon, twisted into a million fearful shapes, swam often before his eyes, as did the sweetly beautiful face of the woman he desired above everything, Yisselda of Brass. Gradually, through an eternity, his whole life began to be built up until he had recalled all that had ever happened to him, everything he had ever thought or dreamed of, not sequentially, but in order of importance. Riding over everything was his desire for Yisselda, his hatred of Hawkmoon and his schemes for ousting Huon from power.

Then the bell was rising and Meliadus looked once again upon the mask of Kalan. For some reason Meliadus felt mentally purged and in high spirits.

"Well, Kalan, what did you discover?"

"Nothing, at this stage, that I did not already know. The full results will take an hour or two to process." He giggled. "The emperor would be much amused to see them."

"Aye. He will not see them, I hope."

"He will see something, Meliadus, that will show that your hatred for Hawkmoon is diminishing and that your love for the emperor is abiding and deep. Do not they tell us that love and hate are close together. Therefore your hatred of Huon will become love, with a little doctoring on my part."

"Good. Now let us discuss the rest of our project. First we must find a way of bringing Castle Brass back to this dimension—or else of finding a way through ourselves—secondly we must discover a means of re-activating the Black Jewel in Hawkmoon's skull and thus getting him into our power again. Lastly we must devise weapons and so forth that will enable us to overcome Huon's forces."

Kalan nodded. "Of course. There are already the new engines I invented for the ships . . ."

"The ships that Trott left with?"

"Aye. The engines drive vessels faster and farther than anything ever before invented. Trott's ships are the only ones so far equipped with them. Trott should be reporting to us soon."

"Where did he go?"

"I am not sure. Only he and King Huon knew—but it must have been a good distance away—several thousand miles at the least. Perhaps to Asiacommunista."

"That seems likely," Meliadus agreed. "Still, let us forget Trott and discuss the details of our plan. Taragorm, also, is working on a device that might help us reach Castle Brass."

"Perhaps it would be best for Taragorm to concentrate on that line of research, since it is his speciality, while I try to find a means of activating the Black Jewel," Kalan suggested.

"Perhaps," murmured Meliadus. "First, I think, I will consult my brother-in-law. I'll leave you now and return shortly."

With that, Meliadus summoned his slaves who brought his litter. He climbed into it, waved farewell to Kalan, and directed the girls to take him to the Palace of Time.

CHAPTER THREE

TARAGORM OF THE PALACE OF TIME

IN TARAGORM'S STRANGE palace, shaped like a gigantic clock, the air was full of clanks and whirrs and the whistling of pendula and balance wheels and Taragorm, in his huge clock mask that told the time as accurately as the other clocks in the palace, took Meliadus's arm and guided him through the Hall of the Pendulum where, a short distance above Meliadus's head, the huge brass bob, made to resemble an ornate, blazing sun, flung its fifty ton weight back and forth across the hall.

"Well, brother," Meliadus shouted above the noise, "you sent me a message that you said I would be pleased to hear, but the message only told me to come to see you."

"Aye. I felt it best to tell you in private. Come." Taragorm led Meliadus through a short passage and into a small room in which stood only one ancient clock. Taragorm closed the door and there was relative silence. He indicated the clock. "It is probably the oldest clock in the world, brother—a 'grandfather' it was called and it was made by Thomas Tompion."

"I have not heard the name."

"A master craftsman—the greatest of his age. He lived well before the onset of the Tragic Miillennium."

"Indeed? And has this something to do with your message?"

"Of course not." Taragorm clapped his hands and a side door opened. A lean, ragged figure stepped through, his face covered by a cracked, plain leather mask. He bowed extravagantly to Meliadus.

"Who is this?"

"It is Elvereza Tozer, brother. You remember the name?"

"Of course! The man who stole Mygan's ring and then vanished!"

"Exactly. Tell my brother Baron Meliadus where you have been, Master Tozer . . ."

Again Tozer bowed and then sat himself down on the edge of the table, spreading his arms wide. "Why, I've been to Castle Brass, my lord!"

Suddenly Meliadus sprang across the room to grab the startled Tozer by the slack of his shirt. "You've been *where*!" he growled.

"C-castle B-Brass, your honour . . ."

Meliadus shook Tozer, lifting him clear of the ground. "How?"

"I reached the place by accident—I was captured by Hawkmoon of Köln—I was held prisoner—my ring taken from me—managed to get ring back—escaped—arrived b-back here . . ." Tozer gasped in fright.

"He brought some information with him that's more interesting," Taragorm said. "Tell him, Tozer."

"The machine that protects them—that keeps them in that other dimension—it's in the dungeons of the castle— kept carefully protected. A crystal thing they got from a place called Soryandum. It's that that took them there and it's that that ensures their safety. It's true, my lord . . ."

Taragorm laughed. "It is true, Meliadus. I've tested him a dozen times. I've heard of this crystal machine but did not suspect it existed still. And with the rest of the information Tozer has given me, I think I can achieve some results."

"You can get us through to Castle Brass?"

"Oh, much more convenient than that, brother—within a short time I am fairly certain that I will bring Castle Brass back to us."

Meliadus looked silently at Taragorm for a moment and then began to laugh. His laughter was so great then that it threatened to drown the noise of the clocks.

"At last! At last! Thank you, brother! Thank you, Master Tozer! Destiny is patently upon my side!"

CHAPTER FOUR

A MISSION FOR MELIADUS

IT WAS ON the following day, however, that Meliadus was summoned to King Huon's Throne Room.

As he made his way to the palace, Meliadus scowled in concentration. Had Kalan betrayed him? Had the scientist told King Huon the true results of the mentality machine's test? Or had King Huon guessed for himself? After all, the monarch was immortal. He had lived for two thousand years and had doubtless learned much. Were Kalan's faked records too clumsy to deceive Huon? Meliadus felt panic rise within him. Was this the end of everything? When he arrived in the Throne Room would Huon order the Mantis Guard to destroy him?

The great gates swung open. The mantis warriors confronted him. At the far end was the Throne Globe, black and mysterious.

Meliadus began to walk towards the Throne Globe.

Eventually he reached it and bowed before it, but for a long while it remained solid, mysterious black. Was Huon playing with him?

At length it began to swirl dark blue, then green, then pink and then white, revealing the foetus shape with its sharp, malevolent eyes staring down at Meliadus.

"Baron . . ."

"Noblest of Rulers."

"We are pleased with you."

Meliadus looked up in astonishment. "Great Emperor?"

"We are pleased with you and we wish to honour you."

"Noble Prince?"

"You know of course that Shenegar Trott left on a special expedition."

"I do, Mighty Monarch."

"And you know where he went."

"I do not, Light of the Universe."

"He went to Amarehk, there to discover what he could

66

about the continent—to see if we should meet resistance if we landed a force there."

"It would seem, then, that he did meet resistance, Immortal Ruler . . .?"

"Aye. He should have reported back a week or more ago. We are concerned."

"You think he is dead, Noble Emperor?"

"We should like to discover that—and also discover who slew him if that is the case. Baron Meliadus. We wish to entrust you with the second expedition."

At first Meliadus was filled with fury. Meliadus play second to that fat buffoon Trott! Meliadus waste time questing about on the coasts of a continent in the hope of discovering Trott's droppings! He would have none of it! He would attack the Throne Globe now, if that senile fool above him would not be sure to have him cut down in an instant. He swallowed his temper and a new scheme began to form in his skull.

"I am honoured, King of All!" he said with mock humility. "Do I choose my crews?"

"If you wish."

"Then I'll take men who I can be sure of. Members of the Order of the Wolf and the Order of the Vulture."

"But these are not sailors. They are not even marines!"

"The Vultures have sailors among them, Emperor of the World, and those are the men I will select."

"As you say, Baron Meliadus, as you say."

Meliadus was astonished to discover that Trott had sailed to Amarehk and it made him even more resentful— for it meant that Huon had entrusted the Count of Sussex with an assignment that was rightfully his. Another score to settle, he told himself. He was glad now that he had bided his time and accepted—or appeared to have accepted—the king's orders. His opportunity, in fact, seemed to have been handed to him by the creature he now considered to be his arch enemy after Hawkmoon.

Meliadus pretended to think for a moment. "If you believe the Vultures to be untrustworthy, Monarch of Space and Time, then may I suggest that I take with me their chief . . .?"

"Their chief? Asrovak Mikosevaar is dead—killed by Hawkmoon!"

"But his widow inherited the Constabulary . . ."

"Flana! A woman!"

"Aye, Great Emperor. She will control them."

"I would not have thought that the Countess of Kanbery could control a rabbit, she is so vague, but if that is your wish, my lord, then so be it."

For a further hour they discussed the details of the plan and the king gave Meliadus all possible information relating to Trott's first expedition.

Then Meliadus left, his hidden eyes full of triumph.

CHAPTER FIVE

THE FLEET AT DEAU-VERE

OVERLOOKED BY THE turreted city of Deau-Vere, flanked on three sides by quays of scarlet stone, the small fleet lay at anchor in a livid sea. On the wide roofs of the buildings stood thousands of ornithopters, fancifully fashioned to resemble birds and mythical beasts, their wings folded; and in the streets below their pilots swaggered in masks of Crow and Owl, mingling with the sailors in their Fish and Sea Serpent helms and the infantry and cavalry—Pig, Skull, Hound, Goat and Bull—who were preparing to cross the Channel not by ship but by the famed Silver Bridge Across The Sea which could be seen on the other side of the city, its great curve disappearing into the distance, all delicate and shining and loaded constantly with traffic coming to and from the Continent.

The men-o'-war in the harbour were crowded with soldiers clad in Wolf and Vulture helms and armed to the teeth with swords, spears, bows, quivers of arrows and flame lances and the flagship bore the banners both of the Grand Constable of the Order of the Wolf and of the Grand Constable of the Order of the Vulture which had once been simply the Vulture Legion but which had been raised to the status of an Order by King Huon, for the fighting it had done in Europe and to honour the death of its bloodthirsty chieftain Asrovak Mikosevaar.

The ships themselves were remarkable in that they had no sails but were instead mounted with huge paddle-wheels at their sterns. They were built of a mixture of wood and metal—the wood ornately carved and the metal wrought in baroque designs. There were panels in their sides, each carrying an intricate painting depicting some earlier sea victory for Granbretan. Gilded figureheads decorated the forward parts of the ships, representing the terrifying ancient gods of Granbretan—*Jhone, Jhorg, Phowl, Rhunga,* who were said to have ruled the land before the Tragic Millennium—*Chirshil,* the Howling God;

Bjrin Adass, the Singing God; *Jeajee Blad,* the Groaning God; *Jh'Im Slas,* the Weeping God and *Aral Vilsn,* the Roaring God, Supreme God, father of *Skvese* and *Blansacredid* the gods of Doom and Chaos.

The *Aral Vilsn* was the flagship and on the flagship's bridge stood the brooding figure of Baron Meliadus, beside him Countess Flana Mikosevaar. Below the bridge the captains of the ships in Wolf and Vulture masks were beginning to assemble, having been summoned to the flagship by Meliadus.

They looked up expectantly as Meliadus cleared his throat.

"You are doubtless wondering about our destination gentlemen—and wondering, too, about the nature of these strange ships we sail in. The ships are no mystery—they are equipped with engines similar to those which power our ornithopters, but much more powerful, and are the invention of that genius of Granbretan, Baron Kalan of Vitall. They can bear us swifter than sail across continents of water and do not need to wait on the will of the elements. As to our destination, that I will reveal in private. This ship is the *Aral Vilsn,* named after the supreme god of ancient Granbretan, who made this nation into what she is today. Her sister ships are the *Skvese* and the *Blansacredid,* which are the old words for Doom and for Chaos. But they are also the sons of *Aral Vilsn* and represent the glory of Granbretan, the old dark glory, the gloomy glory, the bloody and terrible glory of our land. A glory of which I am sure you are all rightly proud." Meliadus paused. "Would you see it lost, gentlemen?"

The answer roared back. *No! No!* By *Aral Vilsn,* by *Skvese* and *Plansacredid—No! N O !"*

"And would you do anything to make sure that Granbretan retained her black might and her lunatic glory?"

"AYE! AYE! AYE!"

"And would you all unite with me in an insane adventure such as those embarked upon by *Aral Vilsn* and his peers?"

"AYE! Tell us what is it! Tell us!"

"You would not shrink from it? You would follow it through to the end?"

"AYE!" shouted more than a score of voices.

"Then follow me to my cabin and I will detail the plan. But be warned, once you have entered that cabin, you will have to follow me forever. Any who holds back will not leave the cabin alive."

Then Meliadus swung down from the bridge and strode into his cabin below it. He was followed by every one of the captains who stood before him and every one of them was to leave the cabin alive.

Baron Meliadus stood before them. His dark cabin was lighted only by a dim lamp. There were maps on his table, but he did not consult them. He spoke in a low, vibrant voice to his men.

"I shall not waste time further, gentlemen, but will tell you at once the nature of this adventure. We are embarking upon treason . . ." He cleared his throat. "We are about to rebel against our hereditary ruler, Huon the King Emperor."

There were many gasps from around the cabin as the Wolf and Vulture masks stared intently at Baron Meliadus.

"King Huon is insane," Meliadus told them quickly. "It is not personal ambition that drives me to this scheme, but a love for our nation. Huon is mad—his two thousand years of life has clouded his brain rather than given him wisdom. He is trying to make us expand too rapidly. This expedition, for instance, was to go to Amarehk to see if the land could be conquered, while we have barely crushed the whole Middle East and there are still parts of Muskovia that are not entirely ours."

"And you would rule in Huon's place, eh, baron?" a Vulture captain suggested cynically.

Meliadus shook his head. "Not at all. Flana Mikosevaar would be your Queen. Vulture and Wolf would take the place of the Mantis in the royal favour. Yours would be the supreme Orders . . ."

"But the Vultures are a mercenary Order," a Wolf captain pointed out.

Meliadus shrugged. "They have proved loyal to Granbretan. And it could be argued that many of our

71

own Orders are moribund, that fresh blood is needed in the Dark Empire."

Another Vulture captain spoke thoughtfully. "So Flana would be our Queen Empress—and you, baron?"

"Regent and Consort. I shall marry Flana and aid her rule."

"You would truly be the King Emperor in all but name," said the same Vulture captain.

"I would be powerful, it is true—but Flana is of the Royal blood, not I. She is your Queen Empress by right of ancestry. I shall be merely Supreme Warlord and leave the other affairs of state to her—for war's my life, gentlemen, and I seek only to improve the manner in which our wars are conducted."

The captains seemed satisfied.

Meliadus continued: "So instead of sailing to Amarehk on the morning tide, we sail around the coast a little, biding our time, then make for the Tayme estuary, sailing upriver to Londra and arriving in the heart of the city before anyone can guess our intent."

"But Huon is well-protected. His palace is impossible to storm. There will be legions in the city loyal to him, surely," said another Wolf captain.

"We will have allies in the city. Many of the legions will be with us. Taragorm is on our side and he is hereditary commander of several thousand warriors since his cousin's death. The Order of the Ferret is a small one, to be sure, but it has many legions in Londra, while other legions are in Europe, defending our possessions. All the nobles likely to remain loyal to Huon are abroad at this moment. It is a perfect time to strike. Baron Kalan is also with us—he can aid us with new weapons and his Serpents to operate them. If we achieve a swift victory—or at least make quick gains—then it is likely that many others will join us, for few will discover love for King Huon once Flana is on the throne."

"I feel a loyalty for King Huon . . ," admitted a Wolf captain. "It is bred into us."

"And so is a loyalty to the spirit of *Aral Vilsn*—to all that Granbretan stands for. Is that not a loyalty even more deeply bred into us?"

The captain deliberated for a moment before nodding.

"Aye—you are right. With a new ruler of the blood royal on the throne, then perhaps our whole greatness will come to us."

"Oh, it will, it will!" promised Meliadus fiercely, his black eyes gleaming from his snarling helm.

CHAPTER SIX

THE RETURN TO CASTLE BRASS

IN THE GREAT hall of Castle Brass Yisselda Hawk-moon, Count Brass's daughter, wept and wept.

She wept for joy, hardly able to believe that the man before her was her husband whom she loved with such passion, hardly daring to touch him lest he prove a phantom. Hawkmoon laughed and strode forward, putting his arms around her and kissing at her tears. Then she, too, began to laugh, her face becoming radiant.

"Oh, Dorian! Dorian! We feared you killed in Gran-bretan!"

Hawkmoon grinned. "Considering everything, Gran-bretan was the safest place we saw in our travels! Is that not so, D'Averc?"

D'Averc coughed into his kerchief. "Aye—and maybe the healthiest, too."

The thin and kindly-faced Bowgentle shook his head in mild astonishment. "But how did you return from Amarekh in that dimension to the Kamarg in this?"

Hawkmoon shrugged his shoulders. "Ask me not, Sir Bowgentle, ask me not. The Great Good Ones brought us here, that is all I know. The journey was swift, taking but a few minutes."

"The Great Good Ones! Never heard of 'em!" Count Brass spoke gruffly, stroking his red mustachios and trying to hide the tears in his eyes. "Spirits of some sort, eh?"

"Aye of some sort, father." Hawkmoon stretched out his hand to his father-in-law. "You are looking well, Count Brass. Your hair's as red as ever."

"That's not a sign of youth," Count Brass complained. "That's rust! I'm rotting here while you enjoy yourself chasing about the world."

Oladahn, the little son of a giantess of the Bulgar Mountains, stepped shyly forward. "I'm glad to see you

back, friend Hawkmoon. And in good health, it seems."
He grinned, offering Hawkmoon a goblet of wine. "Here
—drink this as a welcome cup!"

Hawkmoon smiled back and accepted the goblet,
quaffing it in a single draft. "Thanks, friend Oladahn.
How's it with you?"

"Boring. We are all bored—and afraid you would not
return."

"Well, I am back and I think I have enough stories
of my adventures to dispel your boredom for a few hours.
And I have news of a mission for us all which will bring
you relief from the inactivity you have been suffering."

"Tell us!" Count Brass roared. "For all our sakes—
tell us at once!"

Hawkmoon laughed easily. "Aye—but give me a
moment to look at my wife." He turned and stared into
Yisselda's eyes and he saw that they were now perturbed.

"What is it, Yisselda?"

"I see something in your manner," said she. "Something
that tells me, my lord, that you are soon to risk your
life again."

"Perhaps."

"If it must be, then it must be." She took a deep breath
and smiled at him "But it will not be tonight, I hope."

"Nor for several nights. We have many plans to make."

"Aye," she said softly, glancing at the stones of the
hall. "And I have much to tell you."

Count Brass stepped forward gesturing to the far end
of the hall where the servants were laying the table with
food. "Let's eat. We have saved our best for this home-
coming."

Later as they sat with full bellies by the fire, Hawkmoon
showed them the Sword of the Dawn and the Runestaff,
which he drew from his shirt. At once the hall was
illuminated with whirling flames making patterns in the
air and the strange bitter-sweet scent filled the hall.

The others looked at the thing in silent awe until Hawkmoon replaced it. "That is our standard, my friends. That
is what we now serve when we go out to fight the whole
Dark Empire."

Oladahn scratched at the fur on his face. "The whole Dark Empire, eh?"

Hawkmoon smiled gently. "Aye."

"Are there not several million warriors on the side of Granbretan?" Bowgentle asked innocently.

"There are *several* million, I believe."

"And we have about five hundred Kamargians left at Castle Brass," murmured Count Brass wiping his lips on his sleeve and giving a mock frown. "Let me compute that . . ."

D'Averc now spoke. "We have more than five hundred. You forget the Legion of the Dawn." He pointed at Hawkmoon's sword which lay scabbarded beside his chair.

"How many in that mysterious legion?" Oladahn asked.

"I do not know—perhaps an infinite number, perhaps not."

"Say a thousand," Count Brass mused. "To be conservative of course. Making fifteen hundred warriors against —"

"Several million," supplied D'Averc.

"Aye, several million, equipped with all the resources of the Dark Empire, including scientific knowledge we cannot match . . ."

"We have the Red Amulet and the Rings of Mygan," Hawkmoon reminded him.

"Ah, yes, those . . ." Count Brass seemed to scowl. We have those, too. And we have right on our side—is that an asset, Duke Dorian?"

"Perhaps. But if we use the Rings of Mygan to take us back to our own dimension and we fight a couple of small battles close to home, freeing the oppressed, we can begin to raise some kind of peasant army."

"A peasant army, you say. Hm . . ."

Hawkmoon sighed. "I know it seems impossible odds, Count Brass."

Then Count Brass suddenly broke into a beaming, golden smile. "That's right, lad. You've guessed!"

"What do you mean?"

"They're just the sort of odds I like. I'll get the maps and we can begin to plan our initial campaigns!"

While Count Brass was away, Oladahn said to Hawkmoon. "We forgot to tell you, I suppose, that Elvereza

Tozer escaped. He killed his guard while he was out riding, returned here, recovered his ring and vanished."

Hawkmoon frowned. "That is bad news. He might have returned to Londra."

"Exactly. We are very vulnerable at this moment, friend Hawkmoon."

Count Brass came back with the maps. "Now, let's see . . ."

An hour later Hawkmoon got up and took Yisselda's hand, bid goodnight to his friends and followed his wife to their apartments.

Five hours later they were still awake, lying in each other's arms. It was then that she told him they were to have a child.

He accepted the news in silence, merely kissed her and held her closer. But when she was asleep, he got up and went to the window, staring out over the reeds and lagoons of the Kamarg, thinking to himself that now he had something even more important to fight for than an ideal.

He hoped he would live to see his child.

He hoped his child would be born even if he did not live.

CHAPTER SEVEN

THE BEASTS BEGIN TO SQUABBLE

MELIADUS SMILED BEHIND his mask and his hand tightened on Flana Mikosevaar's shoulder as the towers of Londra came in sight upriver.

"It is going so well," he murmured. "Soon, my dear, you will be Queen. They do not suspect. They cannot suspect. There has been no uprising such as this for a hundred centuries! They are unprepared. How they will curse the architects who sited the barracks on the waterfront!" He laughed softly.

Flana was tired of the thrumming of the engines and the rumble of the paddle wheel as it pushed the ship on its course. One of the virtues of a sailing ship, she now realised, was that it was silent. These noisy things would not be allowed in sight of Londra again once their purpose was served and she ruled. But the irritation was slight and the decision unimportant. Again she turned her thoughts inward and forgot Meliadus and his plan, forgot that the only reason she had agreed to his plan was because she did not care what became of her. She was thinking again of D'Averc.

The captains on board the ships ahead knew what to do. As well as having Kalan's engines, they were now equipped with Kalan's flame cannon and they knew their targets—the military barracks of the Orders of the Pig and the Rat and the Fly and others lining the river close to the outskirts of Londra.

Softly Baron Meliadus instructed his ship's captain to raise the appropriate colour, the flag that would give the signal to begin the bombardment.

Londra was still in the morning, as gloomy as ever, as darkly bizarre as usual, with her crazy towers leaning into the sky, like the clutching fingers of a million madmen.

It was early. None but the slaves would be awake. None, that is, save Taragorm, Kalan and their men, waiting for the sounds of strife so that they could move their men into their positions. The intentions was to slay as many as possible and then drive the rest towards the palace, bottling them in, containing them so that they should have not several objectives but one by the afternoon.

Meliadus knew that even if they succeeded in this plan that the real fighting would begin with the attack on the palace and that they would be hard put to take it before reinforcements arrived.

Meliadus's breathing quickened. His eyes gleamed, from the bronze snouts of the cannon flame spewed, shrieking towards the unsuspecting barracks. Within the first few seconds the morning air was split by a tremendous explosion as one of the barracks blew up.

"What luck!" Meliadus exclaimed. "This is a splendid omen. I had not thought to have such success so soon!"

A second explosion—a barracks on the other side of the water—and from the remaining buildings ran terrified men, some so alarmed that they had even left their masks behind! As they scurried from their barracks the flame cannon caught them, burning them to cinders. Their yells and screams echoed among the sleeping towers of Londra —the first warning that most of the citizens had had.

Wolf mask turned to Vulture helm in expressions of silent satisfaction as they witnessed the carnage on the banks. Pigs and Rats scuttled for cover—Flies flung themselves behind the nearest buildings still standing and the few who had managed to bring flame lances with them began to open fire.

The beasts had started to squabble.

It was part of that pattern of destiny that Meliadus had begun when, on leaving Castle Brass in disgrace, he had called upon the Runestaff.

But none could yet say how that pattern would resolve itself or who would be the ultimate victor—Huon, Meliadus or Hawkmoon.

CHAPTER EIGHT

TARAGORM'S INVENTION

BY MID MORNING the barracks had been completely wiped out and the survivors were fighting in the streets near the centre of the city. They had now been reinforced with several thousand Mantis warriors. It was probable that Huon still had no idea of what was really happening. Perhaps he even thought the attack was by Asiacommunistans disguised as Granbretanians. Meliadus smiled as he disembarked with Flana Mikosevaar and made his way to the Palace of Time on foot, flanked by a dozen Vultures and Wolves. The surprise had been complete. His men had remained in the few open streets and had not ventured into the maze of corridors that linked most of the towers. As the warriors had emerged, Meliadus's men had picked them off. Now they were bottling them in, for there were few windows from which Huon's soldiers could fight. Windows were not a great feature of Londra's architecture, for the Granbretanians had little liking for natural air or daylight. Those windows that there were tended to be placed so high as to be nearly useless to snipers. Even the ornithopters, unequipped for fighting in a city such as Londra, were proving to be a smaller threat than Meliadus had anticipated. He was well pleased as he entered the Palace of Time and discovered Taragorm in a small chamber.

"Brother! Our plans go well—better than I had expected."

"Aye," answered Taragorm with a nod to Flana to whom, like Meliadus, he had been married for a short time. "My Ferrets have hardly needed to do anything as yet. But doubtless they'll be useful in flushing out those who stay in the tunnels: I plan to use them to come up from the enemy from behind as soon as we have properly located the main pockets."

Meliadus nodded his approval. "But you sent a message for me to meet you here. Why is that?"

"I believe I have discovered the means of bringing your friends of Castle Brass back to their natural environment," Taragorm murmured, his voice full of quiet satisfaction.

Meliadus gave a deep groan and it was a moment before Flana realised he was voicing his extreme pleasure. "Oh, Taragorm! At last the rabbits are mine!"

Taragorm laughed. "I am not entirely certain that my machine will work, but I feel it might since it is based on an old formula I discovered in the same book as the one which mentioned the crystal machine of Soryandum. Would you care to see it?"

"Aye! Lead me to it, brother, I beg you!"

"This way."

Taragorm led Meliadus and Flana through two short corridors full of the noise of clocks and arrived at last outside a low door which he opened with a small key.

"In here." He took a torch from the bracket outside and used it to light the dungeon he had opened. "There. It is on roughly the same level as the crystal machine at Castle Brass. Its voice can carry through the dimensions."

"I hear nothing," Meliadus said with some disappointment.

"You hear nothing because there is nothing to hear—in this dimension. But it makes a goodly sound, I guarantee, in some other space and time."

Meliadus moved towards the object. It was like a great brass skeleton clock the size of a man. Its pendulum swung beneath it, working the escapement lever that moved the hands. It had springs and cogs and looked in every respect like an ordinary clock made huge. On its back was mounted a gong-like affair with a striking arm. Even as they watched the hands touched the half-hour and the arm moved slowly up to fall suddenly upon the gong. They could see the gong vibrating but did not hear a whisper of sound.

"Incredible!" whispered Meliadus. "But how does it work?"

"I have still to adjust it a little to ensure that it is operating in exactly the correct dimension of space and time which, with the help of Tozer, I have managed to locate. When midnight comes, our friends at Castle Brass should experience something of an unwelcome surprise."

Meliadus sighed with pleasure. "Oh, noble brother! You shall be the richest and most honoured man in the Empire!"

Taragorm's weird clock mask bowed slightly in recognition of Meliadus's promise. "It is only fitting," he murmured, "but I thank you brother."

"You are sure it will work?"

"If it does not, then I shall not be the richest and most honoured man in the Empire," Taragorm said with some humour. "Doubtless, in fact, you shall see to it that I am rewarded in a less pleasant fashion."

Meliadus flung his arms around his brother-in-law's shoulders. "Do not speak of such a thing, brother! Oh, do not speak of it!"

CHAPTER NINE

HUON CONFERS WITH HIS CAPTAINS

"WELL, WELL, GENTLEMEN. Some sort of civil disturbance, we gather." The gold voice came from the wizened throat and the sharp black eyes darted this way and that at the gathered masks before them.

"It is treason, Noble Monarch," a Mantis mask said. His uniform was untidy and his mask singed by a flame lance.

"Civil war, Great Emperor," another emphasised.

"And very nearly a fait accompli," murmured the man next to him, almost to himself. "We were totally unprepared, Excellent Ruler."

"Indeed you were, gentlemen. Totally. We blame you all—and ourselves. We were deceived."

The eyes moved more slowly over the assembled captains. "And is Kalan amongst you?"

"He is not, Grand Sire."

"And Taragorm?" purred the sweet voice.

"Taragorm is not present, King of All."

"So . . . And some thought you saw Meliadus on the flagship . . ."

"With Countess Flana, Magnificent Emperor."

"That is logical. Yes, we have been very much deceived. But no matter—the palace is well defended, we assume?"

"Only a very large force could possibly hope to take it, Lord of the World."

"But perhaps they have a very large force? And if they have Kalan and Taragorm with them, they have other powers. Were we prepared for siege, captain?" Huon addressed the Captain of the Mantis Guard who bowed his head.

"After a fashion, Excellent Prince. But such a thing is without precedent."

"Indeed it is. Perhaps we should seek reinforcements, then?"

"From the Continent," said a captain. "All the loyal barons are there—Adaz Promp, Brenal Farun, Shenegar Trott . . ."

"Shenegar Trott is not on the Continent," King Huon said politely.

". . . Jerek Nankenseen. Mygel Holst . . ."

"Yes, yes, yes—we know the names of our barons. But can we be sure that these are loyal?"

"I would assume so, Great King Emperor, for their men perished today. If they were in league with Meliadus, they would have given him those loyal to their Order, surely?"

"Your guess is probably accurate. Very well—recall the Lords of Granbretan. Tell them to bring all available troops to squash this uprising as quickly as possible. Tell them that it is inconvenient to us. The messenger had best leave from the roof of the palace. We understand that several ornithopters are available."

From somewhere, muffled and distant, there was a roar as if from a flame cannon and the Throne Room seemed to tremble very slightly.

"Exetremely inconvenient," sighed the King Emperor. "What did you estimate as Meliadus's gains in the past hour?"

"Almost the entire city save the palace, Excellent Monarch."

"I always knew he was the best of my generals."

CHAPTER TEN

ALMOST MIDNIGHT

BARON MELIADUS SAT in his own chambers watching the fires of the city. He especially enjoyed the spectacle of an ornithopter crashing in flames over the palace. The night sky was clear and the stars were bright. It was an exceptionally pleasant evening. To make it perfect he had a quartette of girl slaves, once well-known musicians in their own lands, play him the music of Londen Johne, Granbretan's finest composer.

The counterpoint of explosions, of screams and of the clash of metal was exquisite to Meliadus's ear. He sipped his wine and consulted his maps, humming to the music.

There was a knock on his door and a slave opened it. His Chief of Infantry, Vrasla Beli, entered and bowed.

"Captain Beli?"

"I must report, sir, that we are becoming very short of men. We have achieved a miracle on very few, sir, but we cannot ensure our gains without reinforcements. Either that, or we must regroup . . ."

"Or leave the city altogether and choose the ground on which we fight—is that it, Captain Beli?"

"Exactly, sir."

Meliadus rubbed at his mask. "There are detachments of Wolves, Vultures and even Ferrets on the mainland. Perhaps if they were recalled . . ."

"Would there be time, sir?"

"Well, we should have to make time, captain."

"Aye, sir."

"Offer all prisoners a change of mask," Meliadus suggested. "They can see that we are winning and might wish to change to a new Order."

Beli saluted. "King Huon's palace is superbly defended, sir."

"And it will be superbly taken, captain, I am sure."

The music of Johne continued and the firing continued

and Meliadus felt sure that all was going perfectly. It would take time to capture the palace, but he was confident that it would be taken, Huon destroyed, Flana put in his place and Meliadus the most powerful man in the land.

He glanced at the clock on the wall. It was nearing eleven o'clock. He got up and clapped his hands, silencing the girls. "Fetch my litter," he ordered. "I journey to the Palace of Time."

The same four girls returned with his litter and he climbed in to sink among the cushions.

As they moved slowly along the corridors, Meliadus could still hear the music of the flame cannon, the shouts of men in conflict. Admittedly victory had not yet been accomplished and even if he slew King Huon there might be barons who would not accept Flana as Queen Empress. He would need a few months in which to consolidate—but it would help if he could unite them all into turning their hatred against the Kamarg and Castle Brass.

"Hurry," he called to the naked girls. "Faster! We must not be late!"

If Taragorm's machine worked, then he would have the double advantage of being able to reach his enemies and unite his nation.

Meliadus sighed with pleasure. Everything was working so perfectly.

BOOK THREE

CHAPTER ONE
THE STRIKING OF THE CLOCK

*And now the resolution was imminent. The
Heroes of the Kamarg plotted in Castle Brass
—Baron Meliadus plotted in Taragorm's Palace
of Time—the King Emperor Huon plotted in
his Throne Room—and all the plots that were
made began to influence each other. The
Runestaff, too, centrepiece of the drama, was
beginning to exert its influence upon the
players. And now the Dark Empire was divided
—divided because of Meliadus's hatred of
Hawkmoon whom he had planned to use as
his puppet but who had been strong enough to
turn against him. Perhaps it was then—when
Meliadus had chosen Hawkmoon to use against
Castle Brass—that the Runestaff had made its
first move. It was a tightly woven drama—so
tightly woven that certain threads were close to
snapping . . .*
The High History of the Runestaff

THERE WAS A chill in the air. Hawkmoon drew his
heavy cloak about him and turned his sombre head to
regard his comrades. Each face looked at the table. The
fire in the hall was burning low, but the objects on the
table could be clearly seen.

First there was the Red Amulet, its ruddy light staining
their faces as if with blood. This was Hawkmoon's
strength, giving its owner more than natural energy. Then
there were the crystal Rings of Mygan which could
transport those who wore them through the dimensions.
These were their passports back to their own space and

time. Beside the rings lay the scabbarded Sword of the Dawn. In this lay Hawkmoon's army. And finally, wrapped in a length of cloth, there was the Runestaff, Hawkmoon's standard and his hope.

Count Brass cleared his throat. "Even with all these powerful objects, can we defeat an Empire as great as Granbretan?"

"We have the security of our castle," Oladahn reminded him. "From it we can go through the dimensions at will and return at will. By this means we can fight a prolonged guerilla action until we have worn down the enemy's resistance."

Count Brass nodded. "What you say is true, but I am still doubtful."

"You are used to fighting classic battles, with respect, sir," D'Averc reminded him. D'Averc's pale face was framed by the collar of a dark leather cloak. "And you would be happier with a direct confrontation, drawn up in ranks of lancers, archers, cavalry, infantry and so on. But we have not the men to fight such battles. We must strike from the dark, therefore—from behind, from cover —at least initially."

"You are right, I suppose, D'Averc," sighed Count Brass.

Bowgentle poured wine for them all. "Perhaps we should get to our beds, my friends. There is more planning to do and we should be fresh . . ."

Hawkmoon strode to the far end of the table where the maps had been laid out. He rubbed at the Black Jewel in his forehead. "Aye, we must plan our first campaigns carefully." He studied the map of the Kamarg. "There is a chance that there is a permanent camp surrounding the place where Castle Brass stood—perhaps waiting for its return. It's the sort of thing Meliadus would do."

"But did you not feel that perhaps Meliadus's power is waning?" D'Averc said. "Shenegar Trott seemed to think so."

"If that is the case," Hawkmoon agreed, "then it is possible that Meliadus's legions are now deployed elsewhere, since there seems to be some sort of contention at the Court of Londra as to whether we are very important as a threat or not."

Bowgentle made a movement to speak but then cocked his head to one side. Now they all felt a slight tremor run through the floor.

"It's damn' cold," Count Brass grumbled and went to the fire to fling on another log. Sparks flew and the log caught quickly, the flames sending red shadows skipping through the hall. Count Brass had wrapped his bull-like body in a simple woollen robe and now he tugged at this as if regretting he had not worn something more substantial. He glanced at the rack at the far end of the hall. The rack contained spears, bows, arrows, maces, swords —and his own broadsword, and his armour of brass. His great, bronzed face was clouded.

Again a tremor shook the building and the arms decorating the walls rattled.

Hawkmoon glanced at Bowgentle, noticing in his eyes the same sense of inexplicable doom that he felt. "A mild earthquake, perhaps?"

"Perhaps," murmured Bowgentle, plainly unconvinced.

Now they heard a sound—a distant sound like the booming of a gong, so low as to be almost inaudible. They rushed to the doors of the hall and Count Brass hesitated for a moment before flinging them open and looking up at the night.

They sky was black, but the clouds seemed dark blue, swirling in considerable agitation as if the dome of the sky was about to crack.

Now the reverberation came again, this time plainly audible. The voice of a huge, low bell or a gong that hummed in their ears.

"It is like being in the bell-tower of the castle as the clock strikes," Bowgentle said, his eyes full of alarm.

Every face was pale—every face tense. Hawkmoon began to stride back into the hall, walking with arm out-stretched towards the Sword of the Dawn. D'Averc called to him. "What do you suspect, Hawkmoon? Some kind of attack by the Dark Empire?"

"By the Dark Empire—or by something supernatural," Hawkmoon answered.

A third stroke sounded filling the night, echoing over the flat marshes of the Kamarg, over the lagoons and the reeds. Flamingoes, disturbed by the noise, began to squawk from the darkness.

A fourth followed, louder still—a great booming bell of doom.

A fifth. And Count Brass went to the rack and took up his broadsword.

A sixth. D'Averc covered his ears as the sound increased. "This is sure to bring on at least a mild migraine," he complained languidly.

A seventh. Yisselda ran down the stairs in her night-clothes. "What is it, Dorian? Father—what's the sound? It is like the striking of a clock. It threatens to burst my eardrums . . ."

Oladahn looked up gloomily. "It seems to me that it threatens our very existence," he said. "Though I do not know why I think that . . ." A seventh stroke sounded and plaster fell from the ceiling as the castle shook to its foundations.

"We had better close the doors," Count Brass said as the echo died sufficiently for him to make himself heard. Slowly they moved inside and Hawkmoon helped Count Brass push the doors together and replace the heavy iron bar.

An eighth stroke that filled the hall and made them all press their palms to their ears. A huge shield, there from time immemorial, clattered from the wall, fell to the flag-stones and rolled about noisily until it came to rest near the table.

The servants were running into the hall now. They were plainly in a panic.

A ninth stroke and windows cracked, the glass splinter-ing and crashing to the ground. This time Hawkmoon felt as if he were on a ship at sea that had struck suddenly a hidden reef, for the whole Castle shuddered and they were flung about. Yisselda began to fall, but Hawkmoon just managed to save her, hanging on to a pillar to stop himself from toppling. The sound made him feel sick and his vision was blurred.

For the tenth time the great gong reverberated, as if the whole world shook, as if the universe itself was filled with the sound that signalled the end of everything.

Bowgentle keeled over and fell upon the flagstones in

a faint. Oladahn reeled about, his palms pressing at his head, staggered and collapsed to the floor. Hawkmoon clung to Yisselda grimly, barely able to retain his grip. He was filled with nausea and his head pounded. Count Brass and D'Averc had staggered across the room to the table and were hanging on to it as it shook. As the stroke died Hawkmoon heard D'Averc call: "Hawkmoon—look at this!"

Supporting Yisselda, Hawkmoon managed to reach the table and stared down at the Rings of Mygan. He gasped. Every one of the crystals had shattered.

"So much for our scheme of guerilla raids," D'Averc said hoarsely. "So much, perhaps, for all our schemes ..."

The eleventh stroke sounded. It was deeper and louder than the one before and the whole castle shuddered and flung them to the floor. Hawkmoon screamed in pain as the sound roared in his skull and seemed to sear his brain, but he could not hear his scream above the noise. Everything was shaking and he rolled about on the floor at the mercy of whatever force it was that made the castle quake.

As it faded, he crawled on his hands and knees towards Yisselda, desperately trying to reach her. Tears of pain streamed down his face and he knew by the warmth that his ears were bleeding. Dimly he saw Count Brass trying to rise by clutching at the table. The count's ears gouted gore that matched his hair. "We are destroyed," he heard the old man say: "Destroyed by some cowardly enemy that we cannot even see! Destroyed by a force against which our swords are useless!"

Hawkmoon continued to crawl towards Yisselda who lay prone on the floor.

Now the twelfth stroke sounded, louder and more terrible than the rest. The stones of the castle threatened to crack. The wood of the table split and the thing collapsed with a crash. Flagstones suddenly broke in twain or shattered to fragments. The castle was tossed like a cork in a gale and Hawkmoon roared with pain as the tears in his eyes were now replaced with blood, as the veins in his body threatened to burst.

Then the deep note was counterpointed by another— a high-pitched scream—and colours began to flood the hall. First came violet, then purple, then black. A million tiny bells seemed to ring in unison and this time it was possible to locate the sound as it came from below them, from the dungeons.

Weakly, Hawkmoon attempted to rise and then fell face down on the stones. The note boomed gradually away, the colours began to fade, the ringing sound subsided quite suddenly.

Soon there was silence.

CHAPTER TWO

THE BLACKENED MARSH

"THE CRYSTAL IS destroyed . . ."

Hawkmoon shook his head and blinked his eyes. "Eh?"

"The crystal is destroyed," D'Averc knelt beside him trying to help him to his feet.

"Yisselda?" Hawkmoon said. "How is she?"

"No worse than you. We have put her to bed. The crystal is destroyed."

Hawkmoon dug dried blood from his ears and nostrils. "You mean the Rings of Mygan?"

"D'Averc—tell him more clearly." It was Bowgentle's voice. "Tell him that the machine of the wraith folk is broken."

"Broken?" Hawkmoon heaved himself to his feet. "Was that the final shattering sound I heard?"

"That was it." Now Count Brass stood nearby, leaning wearily on a table and mopping at his face. "The vibrations destroyed the crystals."

"Then—?" Hawkmoon glanced questioningly at Count Brass who nodded.

"Aye—we're back in our own dimension."

"And not under attack?"

"It does not seem so."

Hawkmoon drew a deep breath and began to walk slowly to the main doors of the hall. Painfully he drew back the iron bar and tugged the doors open.

It was still night. The stars in the sky remained the same but the swirling blue clouds had vanished and there was an uncanny silence hanging over the area, a strange smell in the air. But no flamingoes squawked, no wind sighed through the reeds.

Slowly, thoughtfully, Hawkmoon closed the doors again.

"Where are the legions?" D'Averc asked. "One would have thought they were waiting for us—at least a few!"

Hawkmoon frowned. "We'll have to wait until morning before we can guess the answer to that. Perhaps they are out there. planning to take us by surprise."

"Do you think that sound that came was sent by the Dark Empire?" Oladahn asked.

"'Without doubt it did," Count Brass answered. "They have succeeded in their object. They have brought us back to our own dimension." He sniffed the air. "I wish I could identify that smell."

D'Averc was sorting things from the wreckage of the table. "It is a miracle that we are alive," he said.

"Aye," said Hawkmoon. "That noise seemed to affect inanimate things worse than us."

"Two of the older servants are dead," Count Brass said quietly. "Their hearts could not stand it, I suppose. They are being buried now, in case it is not possible in the morning. In the inner courtyard."

"What of the castle?" Oladahn asked.

Count Brass shrugged. "It's hard to tell. I've been down to the dungeons. The crystal machine is completely smashed and some of the stonework is cracked. But this is a strong old castle. She seems to have fared not too badly. No window glass, of course. No glass of any sort intact. Otherwise . . ." He shrugged as if his beloved castle had ceased to matter to him, ". . . otherwise we are still standing as firm as we did before."

"Let's hope so," murmured D'Averc. He held the Sword of the Dawn by its scabbard and the Red Amulet by its chain. He offered them to Hawkmoon. "You'd best don these for it is certain that you will soon have need of them."

Hawkmoon put the amulet around his neck and buckled the scabbard to his belt. Then he stopped and picked up the swaddled Runestaff.

"This does not seem to be bringing us the luck I had hoped," he said and sighed.

Dawn came at last. It came slowly and it came grey and chill, the horizon white as an old corpse and the clouds the colour of bone.

Five heroes watched it rise. They stood outside the gates of Castle Brass, on the hill, and their hands were on their swords, their grips tightening as the saw the scene below.

It was the Kamarg they had left, but it was a Kamarg wasted by war. The smell they had spoken of earlier was the smell of carnage, of a burnt land. For as far as they could see, all was black ruin. The marshes and lagoons had all been dried up by the fire of the flame cannon. The flamingoes, the horses and the bulls had been destroyed or fled. The watchtowers that had guarded the borders were flattened. It seemed as if the whole world was a sea of grey ash.

"It is all gone," said Count Brass in a low voice. "All gone, my beloved Kamarg, my people, my animals. I was their elected Lord Guardian and I failed in my task. Now there is nothing to live for save vengeance. Let me reach the gates of Londra and see the city taken. Then I will die. But not before."

CHAPTER THREE

DARK EMPIRE CARNAGE

BY THE TIME they reached the borders of the Kamarg, Hawkmoon and Oladahn were covered from head to foot in clinging ash that stung their nostrils and was harsh in their throats. Their horses, too, were covered in the stuff and their eyes were as red as their riders'.

Now the sea of ash gave way to sparse, yellow grassland and still they had found no sign that the legions of the Dark Empire occupied the land,

A little watery sunshine broke through the layers of cloud as Hawkmoon drew his horse to a halt and consulted his map. He pointed due East. "The village of Verlin lies yonder. Let's ride cautiously and see if Granbretanian troops still occupy it."

The village came in sight at last and when he saw it Hawkmoon began to gallop faster. Oladahn called from behind him:

"What is it, Duke Dorian? What has happened?"

Hawkmoon did not reply for, as they neared the village, it could be seen that half the buildings lay in ruins, that corpses choked the streets. And still no sign that the Dark Empire troops remained here.

Many of the buildings had been blackened by flame lance fire and some of the corpses bore the signs that they had been slain by flame lances. Here and there lay the body of a Granbretanian, an armoured figure with its mask tilting skyward.

"They were all Wolves here, by the look of it," Hawkmoon murmured. "Meliadus's men. It seems they fell upon the villagers and the villagers attacked them back. See—that Wolf was stabbed by a reaping hook—that one died from the blow of the spade still in his neck . . ."

"Maybe the villagers rose up against them," Oladahn suggested, "and the Wolves retaliated."

"Then why did they leave the village?" Hawkmoon pointed out. "They were garrisoned here."

They guided their horses over the bodies of the fallen. The stink of death was still heavy in the air. It was plain that this carnage had been wreaked only recently. Hawkmoon pointed out gutted stores and the corpses of cattle, horses, even dogs.

"They left nothing alive. Nothing that could be used for food. It is as if they were in retreat from some more powerful enemy!"

"Who is more powerful than the Dark Empire?" Oladahn said with a shudder. "Have we some new enemy to face, friend Hawkmoon?"

"I hope not. Yet this sight is puzzling."

"And disgusting," Oladahn added. There were not only men dead in the streets, but children too and every woman, young or old, bore signs of having been raped before she had been slain, mostly by means of a cut throat, for the Granbretanian soldiery liked to slay their victims as they raped them.

Hawkmoon sighed. "It is the sign of the Dark Empire, everywhere you venture."

He looked up, bending his head to catch a small sound carried on the chill wind. "A cry! Someone still lives, perhaps."

He turned his horse and followed the sound until he entered a sidestreet. Here a door had been broken open and a girl's body lay half in the doorway, half in the street. The cry was stronger. Hawkmoon dismounted and walked cautiously towards the house. It came from the girl. Quickly he knelt down and raised her in his arms. She was almost naked, her body covered with a few strips of torn clothing. There was a red line across her throat as if a blunt dagger had been drawn across it. She was about fifteen, with tangled fair hair and glazed blue eyes. Her body was a mass of blue-black bruises. She gasped as Hawkmoon lifted her.

Hawkmoon lowered her gently and went to his saddle, returning with a flask of wine. He put the flask to her lips and she drank, gasping, her eyes suddenly widening in alarm.

"Do not fear," Hawkmoon said softly. "I am an enemy of the Dark Empire."

"And you live?"

Hawkmoon smiled sardonically. "Aye—I live. I am Dorian Hawkmoon, the Duke of Köln."

"Hawkmoon von Köln? But we thought you dead—or flown forever . . ."

"Well I have returned and your village shall be revenged, I swear. What happened here?"

"I am not altogether sure, my lord, save that the beasts of the Dark Empire intended to leave none alive." She looked up suddenly. "My father and mother—my sister . . ."

Hawkmoon glanced inside the house and shuddered. "Dead," he said. It had been an understatement. They had been disgustingly mutilated. He picked up the girl as she sobbed and took her to his horse. "I will carry you back to Castle Brass," he said.

CHAPTER FOUR

NEW HELMS

SHE LAY IN the softest bed in Castle Brass, tended by Bowgentle, comforted by Yisselda and Hawkmoon who sat beside her bed. But she was dying. She was dying not so much from her injuries as from sorrow. She wished to die. They respected that wish.

"For several months," she murmured, "the Wolf troops occupied our village. They took everything while we starved. We heard that they were part of an army left to guard the Kamarg, though we could not think what there was to guard of that wasteland . . ."

"They were awaiting our return most likely," Hawkmoon told her.

"That would seem likely," the girl said gravely.

She continued: "Then yesterday an ornithopter arrived at the village and its pilot went straight to the commander of the garrison. We heard it rumoured that the soldiers were being recalled to Londra and we were overjoyed. An hour later the soldiers of the garrison fell upon the village, killing, looting, raping. They had orders to leave nothing alive so that when they returned they would not meet resistance, so that any others who came upon the village should not find food. An hour afterwards, they were gone."

"So they plan to return," Hawkmoon mused. "But I wonder why they left . . ."

"Some invading enemy, perhaps?" Bowgentle suggested, bathing the girl's brow.

"That was my guess—and yet it does not seem to fit." Hawkmoon sighed. "It is puzzling—frightening that we know so little."

There came a knock upon the door and D'Averc entered. "An old friend is here, Hawkmoon."

"An old friend? Who?"

"The Orkneyman—Orland Fank."

Hawkmoon rose. "Perhaps he can enlighten us."

As he walked towards the door Bowgentle said quietly. "The girl is dead, Duke Dorian."

"She knows she will be avenged," Hawkmoon said flatly and he left to descend the stairs to the hall.

"Something is in the wind, I agree, friend," Orland Fank was saying to Count Brass as they stood together beside the fire. He waved his hand as Hawkmoon joined them. " And how d'you fare, Duke Dorian?"

"Well enough, in the circumstances. Do you know why the legions are leaving, Master Fank?"

"I was telling the good Count Brass here that I do not . . ."

"Ah, and I though you omniscient, Master Fank."

Fank grinned sheepishly, tugging off his bonnet to wipe his face with it. "I still need time to gather information and I've been busy the while since you left Dnark. I've brought gifts for all the heroes of Castle Brass."

"You are kind."

"They're not from me, you understand, but from—well, the Runestaff, I suppose. I'll give you them later. They've little practical use, you might think, but then it's hard to say what is practical and what is not in the fight against the Dark Empire.

Hawkmoon turned to D'Averc. "What did you discover on your ride?"

"Much the same as you." D'Averc replied. "Razed villages, all the inhabitants hastily slain. Signs of an over-swift departure on the part of the troops. I gather that there are still some garrisons in the large towns, but they are skeleton staffed—mainly artillery and no cavalry at all."

"This seems insane," murmured Count Brass.

"If they are insane, then we may yet take advantage of their lack of rationality," Hawkmoon said with a grim smile.

"Well spoken, Duke Dorian," Fank clapped his red, brawny hand on Hawkmoon's shoulder. " Now can I bring in the gifts."

"By all means, Master Fank."

"Lend me a couple of servants to help, if you will, for there's six of 'em and they're powerful heavy. I brought them on two horses."

A few moments later the servants came in, each holding two wrapped objects, one in each hand. Fank himself brought in the remaining two. He laid them on the flagstones at their feet. "Open them, gentlemen."

Hawkmoon bent and pulled back the cloth that wrapped one of the gifts. He blinked as the light struck his eyes and he saw his own face reflected perfectly back at him. He was puzzled, dragging off the rest of the cloth to stare in astonishment at the object before him. The others, too, were murmuring in surprise.

The objects were battle helmets designed to cover the whole head and rest on the shoulders. The metal of their manufacture was unfamiliar, but it was polished more finely than the finest mirror Hawkmoon had ever seen. With the exception of two eye slits the fronts of the helms were completely smooth, without decoration of any sort so that whoever stared at them saw a complete image of himself. The backs were crested in the same metal, with clean, simple decoration that showed them to be the work of something more than a craftsman. It suddenly struck Hawkmoon how useful they could be in battle, for the enemy would be confused by his own reflection, would have the impression that he was fighting himself!

Hawkmoon laughed aloud. "Why, whoever invented these must be a genius! They are the finest helms I have ever seen."

"Try them on," Fank said, grinning back. "You'll find they fit well. They are the Runestaff's answer to the beast masks of the Dark Empire."

"How do we know which is ours," Count Brass said.

"You will know," Fank told him. "The one you have opened. The one with the crest the colour of brass."

Count Brass smiled and lifted the helm to place it upon his shoulders. Hawkmoon looked at him and saw his own face, the dull black jewel in the centre of his forehead, staring back in amused surprise. Hawkmoon lifted his own helm over his head. His had a golden crest. Now when he turned to regard Count Brass it seemed at first that the count's helm gave no reflection, until Hawkmoon realised that there were an infinity of reflections.

The others had put their helms on their shoulders.

D'Averc's had a blue crest and Oladahn's a scarlet one. They laughed with pleasure.

"A goodly gift, Master Fank," Hawkmoon said, removing his helmet. "An excellent gift. But what of the other two helms?"

Fank smiled mysteriously. "Ah—ah, yes—they would be for those who would desire them."

"For yourself?"

"Not for myself, no—I must admit I tend to disdain armour. It is cumbersome stuff and it makes it harder for me to wield my old battle-axe here." He jerked his thumb behind him at the axe which was secured by a cord on his back.

"Then who are the other two helms for?" Count Brass said, removing his own helm.

"You will know when you know," Fank said. "And then it will seem obvious to you. How are the folk of Castle Brass faring?"

"You mean the villagers of the hill?" Hawkmoon said. "Well, some of them were slain by the striking of that great gong that recalled us to our own dimension. A few buildings fell, but all in all they survived well enough. All the remaining Kamargian cavalry has survived."

"About five hundred men," said D'Averc. "Our army."

"Aye," Fank said with a sidelong glance at the Frenchman. "Aye. Well, I must be away about my business."

"And what business would that be, Master Fank?" Oladahn asked.

Fank paused. "In the Orkneys, my friend, we do not ask of each other's business," he said chidingly.

"Thank you for the gifts," Oladahn said with a bow, "and forgive my curiosity."

"I accept your apology," Fank said.

"Before you leave, Master Fank, I thank you on behalf of us all for these welcome gifts," Count Brass told him. "And could we bother you with a final question?"

"You are all prone to too much questioning in my own opinion," Fank said. "But then we're close-mouthed folk in the Orkneys. Ask away, friend, and I'll do my level best to answer, if the question is not too personal, that is."

"Do you know how the crystal machine came to be shattered?" Count Brass asked. "What caused it?"

"I would gather that Lord Taragorm, Master of the Palace of Time in Londra, discovered the means of breaking your machine once he understood its source. He has many old texts which would tell him such things. Doubtless he built a clock whose striking would travel through the dimensions and be of such a pitch and volume as to shatter the crystal. It was, I believe, the one remedy of the enemies of the folk of Soryandum who gave you the machine."

"So it was the Dark Empire that brought us back," Hawkmoon said. "But if that was so, then why were they not waiting for us?"

"Perhaps a domestic crisis of some sort," Orland Fank said. "We shall see. Farewell, my friends. I have the feeling we will meet again shortly."

FIVE HEROES AND A HEROINE

As THE GATES closed behind Fank, Bowgentle descended the stairs and there was an odd expression on his kindly features. He walked stiffly, and his eyes had a distant look.

"What is it, Bowgentle," Count Brass said in concern, moving forward to grip his old friend by the arm. "You seem disturbed."

Bowgentle shook his head. "Not disturbed—resolute. I have reached a decision. It is many years since I have wielded a weapon larger than a pen, borne anything weightier than a difficult problem in philosophy. Now I will bear arms against Londra. I will ride with you when you set out against the Dark Empire."

"But Bowgentle," Hawkmoon said, "you are not a warrior. You comfort us, sustain us with your kindness and your wisdom. All these things give us strength and are as useful as any comrade in arms."

"Aye—but this fight will be the last fight, win or lose," Bowgentle reminded him. "If you do not return, then you'll have no need of wisdom—and if you do return, you'll have but little inclination to seek my advice, for you'll be the men who broke the Dark Empire. So I will take up a blade. One of yonder mirror helms will fit me, I know. The one with the black crest"

He stood aside as Bowgentle went to the helm and picked it up. Slowly he lowered it over his head. It fitted perfectly. Reflected in the helm they could see what Bowgentle saw—their own faces at once admiring and grim.

D'Averc was the first to step forward with his hand outstretched. "Very well, Bowgentle. It will be a pleasure to ride with someone of sophisticated wit for a change!"

Hawkmoon frowned. "It is agreed. If you wish to, Bowgentle, we shall all be happier for your riding with us. But who is the other helm for, I wonder?"

"It is for me."

The voice was low, firm, sweet. Hawkmoon turned slowly to stare at his wife.

"No, it is not for you, Yisselda . . ."

"How can you be sure?"

"Well . . ."

"Look at it—the helm with the white crest. Is it not smaller than the others. Suitable for a boy—or a woman."

"Aye," Hawkmoon answered reluctantly.

"And am I not Count Brass's daughter?"

"You are."

"And cannot I ride as well as any of you?"

"You can."

"And did I not fight in the bullring as a girl—and win honour there? And did I not train with the guardians of the Kamarg in the arts of the axe, the sword and the flame lance? Father?"

"It is true, she was proficient in all these arts," Count Brass said soberly. "But proficiency is not all that is required of a warrior . . ."

"Am I not strong?"

"Aye—for a woman . . ." answered the Lord of Castle Brass. "Soft and as strong as silk, I believe a local poet said," he glanced sardonically at Bowgentle, who blushed.

"Is it stamina, then, that I lack?" Yisselda asked, her eyes flashing with a mixture of defiance and humour.

"No—you have more than enough stamina," Hawkmoon said.

"Courage? Do I lack courage?"

"There is none more courageous than you, my child," Count Brass agreed.

"Then what quality do I lack that a warrior has?"

Hawkmoon shrugged his shoulders. "None, Yisselda—save that you are a woman and—and . . ."

"And women do not fight. They merely remain at the fireside to mourn their lost kin, is that it?"

"Or welcome them back . . ."

"Or welcome them back. Well, I have no patience with that scheme of things. Why should I remain behind at Castle Brass. Who will protect me?"

"We will leave guards."

"A few guards—guards that you will need in your

105

battle. You know very well that you will want every man with you."

"Aye, that's true," Hawkmoon said. "But there is one other factor, Yisselda. Do you forget that you carry our child?"

"I do not forget. I carry our child. Aye, and I'll carry it into battle—for if we are defeated there will be nothing for it to inherit save disaster—and if we win then it will know the thrill of victory even before it comes into the world. But if we are all slain—then we shall die together. I'll not be Hawkmoon's widow and I'll not bear Hawkmoon's orphan. I will not be safe at Castle Brass alone, Dorian, I'll ride with you." She went to the mirror helm with the white crest and she picked it up. She drew it over her head and spread her soft arms triumphantly.

"See—it fits perfectly. It was plainly made for me. We will ride together, the six of us, and lead the Kamargians against the massed might of the Dark Empire—five heroes—and, I hope, one heroine!"

"So be it," murmured Hawkmoon moving forward to embrace his wife. "So be it."

CHAPTER SIX

A NEW ALLY

THE WOLVES AND the Vultures had fought their way back from the Continent and were now pouring into Londra. Coming into Londra, too, were the Flies, the Rats, the Goats and the Hounds and all the other bloodthirsty beasts of Granbretan.

From a high tower which was now his command headquarters, Meliadus of Kroiden watched them arrive, flooding in by every gate and battling as they came. One group puzzled him and he strained his eyes to see it better. It was a large detachment of troops riding under a black and white striped banner signifying neutrality. The banner carried beside it now became easier to see.

Meliadus frowned.

The banner was that of Adaz Promp, Grand Constable of the Order of the Hound. Did the neutral flag mean that he had not yet decided on whose side to fight? Or did it mean he planned a complicated trick? Meliadus rubbed his lips thoughtfully. With Adaz Promp on his side he could begin an assault on the palace itself. He reached for his wolf helm and stroked the metal head.

For the past few days as the battle for Londra had reached deadlock Meliadus had become pensive—the more so because he did not know if Taragorm's device had succeeded and brought Castle Brass back to its own dimension. His earlier good humour, based on his success in the initial fighting, had been replaced by a nervousness resulting from several uncertainties.

The door opened. Automatically Meliadus reached for his helm, donning it as he turned.

"Ah, it's you, Flana. What do you want?"

"Taragorm is here."

"Taragorm, eh? Has he something positive to tell me."

The clock mask appeared behind Flana's heron mask.

"I had hoped that you would have some positive news, brother," Taragorm said acidly. "After all, we have made no great gains for the past few days."

"The reinforcements are arriving," Meliadus said petulantly, waving his gauntletted hand at the window. "Wolves and Vultures pouring in—and even some Ferrets."

"Aye—reinforcements for Huon, too—and seemingly in larger numbers than ours."

"Kalan should have his new weapons ready soon," Meliadus said defensively. "They will give us an advantage."

"If they work." Taragorm spoke sardonically. "I am beginning to wonder if I have not made a mistake, joining you."

"It is too late now, brother. We must not quarrel, or we're finished."

"Aye, it's too late, that I'll grant you. Whatever happens, if Huon wins we're all doomed."

"Huon will not win."

"We need a million men to attack the palace and succeed."

"We'll find a million men. If only we can make a little headway, others will come over to our side."

Taragorm ignored this statement and turned instead to Flana. "It is a shame, Flana. You would have made a beautful queen . . ."

"She will still make a queen," Meliadus said savagely, restraining himself from striking Taragorm. "Your pessimism amounts to treachery, Taragorm!"

"And will you slay me for my treachery, brother? With all my knowledge. Only I know all the secrets of Time."

Meliadus shrugged. "Of course I will not slay you. Let us cease this arguing and concentrate instead on winning the palace."

Bored by the quarrel, Flana left the room.

"I must see Kalan," Meliadus said. "He has suffered a setback, having to remove all his equipment to a new site so hastily. Come, Taragorm, we'll visit him together."

They summond their litters, climbed in and had their slaves carry them through the dimly lit corridors of the

tower, down twisting ramps to the rooms that Kalan
had adapted as laboratories. A door opened and foul-
smelling heat struck their bodies. Meliadus could feel it
through his mask. He coughed as he left his litter and
walked in to the chamber where Kalan stood, his scrawny
body naked to the waist and only his mask on his head,
supervising the serpent-masked scientists who toiled for
him.

Kalan greeted them impatiently. "What do you want?
I have no time for conversation!"

"We wondered what progress you were making, baron,"
Meliadus yelled over the boiling sound.

"Good progress, I hope. The facilities are ridiculously
primitive. The weapon is almost ready."

Taragorm glanced at the tangle of tubes and wires
from which all the noise and heat and stink was issuing.
"That's a weapon?"

"It will be, it will be."

"What will it do?"

"Bring me men to mount it on our roof and I'll show
you in a few hours."

Meliadus nodded. "Very well. You realise what depends
on your success, Kalan?"

"Aye, that I do. I'm beginning to curse myself for
joining you, Meliadus, but I'm in with you now and can
only continue. Please leave—I'll send word when the
weapon's ready."

Meliadus and Taragorm walked back through the
corridors, their litters following behind.

"I hope Kalan has not lost all sanity," Taragorm said
icily. "For if he has, that thing might destroy us all."

"Or destroy nothing at all," Meliadus said gloomily.

"Now who is the pessimist, brother?"

Returning to his apartments, Meliadus discovered that
he had a visitor. A fat visitor clad in gaudy silk-covered
armour with a brightly painted helm that represented
a savage and grinning hound.

"Baron Adaz Promp," said Flana Mikosevaar, emerg-
ing from another room. "He arrived shortly after you
left, Meliadus."

"Baron," Meliadus said, bowing formally. "I am honoured."

Adaz Promp's smooth tones came from the helm. "What are the issues, Meliadus? What are the goals?"

"The issues—our plans of conquest. The goals—to put a more rational monarch on the throne of Granbretan. One who will respect the advice of experienced warriors such as ourselves."

"Respect your advice, you mean," Promp chuckled. "Well, I have to admit that I thought you insane, my lord, not Huon. Your pursuing this wild vendetta against Hawkmoon and Castle Brass, for instance. I suspected that it was motivated only by your private lust and vengeance."

"You no longer believe that?"

"I do not care. I am beginning to share your opinion that they represent the greatest danger to Granbretan and that they should be exterminated before we think of anything else."

"Why have you changed your mind, Adaz?" Meliadus leaned forward eagerly. "Why? You have some evidence not known to me?"

"More a suspicion or two," Adaz Promp said slowly, fatly. "A hint of this, a hint of that."

"What sort of hints?"

"A ship we encountered and boarded in the northern seas as we were returning from Scandia to answer our emperor's call. A rumour from France. Nothing more."

"What of the ship? What ship was it?"

"One like those anchored on the river—with the strange contraption on its arse and no sails. It was battered, drifting and had two men aboard, both wounded. They died before we could transfer them to our own vessel."

"Shenegar Trott's ship. From Amarehk."

"Aye—that's what they told us."

"But what has it to do with Hawkmoon?"

"It appears they met Hawkmoon in Amarehk. It seems they received their wounds from Hawkmoon in some bloody battle in a city called Dnark. According to these men—and they were raving—the issue of the dispute was the Runestaff itself."

"And Hawkmoon won the dispute."

110

"Indeed he did. There were a thousand of them, we were told—Trott's men, that is—and only four, including Hawkmoon, against them."

"And Hawkmoon won!"

"Aye—aided by supernatural warriors according to the one who lived long enough to babble the tale. It all sounds like truth mixed with fantasy, but it is plain that Hawkmoon defeated a force much larger than his own and that he personally slew Shenegar Trott. It does seem, also, that he has certain scientific powers at his disposal of which we know little. This is confirmed by the manner in which they managed to escape from us the last time. Which brings me to my second tale, picked up from one of your own Wolves as we marched to Londra."

"What's that,"

"He had heard that Castle Brass has reappeared, that Hawkmoon and the rest took a town to the north of the Kamarg and destroyed every man of ours that occupied it. It's a rumour and hard to believe. Where could Hawkmoon have raised an army at such short notice?"

"Such rumours are common in times of war," Meliadus mused, "but it is possible. Then you now believe that Hawkmoon is a larger threat to us than Huon thought?"

"It's a guess—but I feel it's an informed one. But I'm motivated by other considerations, Meliadus. I think that the sooner we end this fight the better, for if Hawkmoon has an army—recruited, perhaps, in Amarehk—then the sooner we should clear it up. I'm with you, Meliadus. I can put half a million Hounds at your disposal within the next day."

"Have you enough now to take the palace with those that I command?"

"Possibly, if we can have artillery cover."

"That you shall have."

Meliadus pumped Promp's hand. "Oh, Baron Adaz, I believe we shall have victory by the morrow!"

"But how many of us will be alive to see it, I wonder," Promp said. "To take the palace will cost a few thousand lives—perhaps even a few hundred thousand."

"It will be worth it, baron. Believe me, it will be worth it."

Meliadus felt his spirits rising first at the prospect of victory over Huon, but mainly over the chance that he soon might have Hawkmoon in his power again—particularly if Kalan could really find a way of re-activating the Black Jewel as he had promised he would.

CHAPTER SEVEN

THE BATTLE FOR HUON'S
PALACE

MELIADUS WATCHED THEM mount the contraption on the roof of his headquarters. They were high above the streets and close to the palace where the fighting raged. Promp had not yet brought up his Hounds but was waiting to see what Kalan's machine would do before he made an open attack on the palace gates. The huge building seemed capable of withstanding any attack— it looked as if it could survive the end of the world. It rose, tier upon magnificent tier, into the lowering sky. Flanked by four vast towers that glowed with a peculiar golden light, encrusted with grotesque bas-reliefs depicting Granbretan's ancient glory, shining with a million clashing colours, protected by gigantic gates of steel thirty foot thick, the palace appeared to look down contemptuously at the embattled factions.

Even Meliadus felt momentary doubt as he stared at it, then returned his attention to Kalan's weapon. From the mass of wires and tubes projected a great funnel, like the bell of a monstrous trumpet and this was turned toward the palace walls which were crowded with hosts of soldiers, primarily of the Orders of the Mantis, the Pig and the Fly. Outside the city the ranks of other Orders were preparing to assault Meliadus's forces from the rear and he knew that the time element was crucial, that if he won a victory at the palace gates he could hope that others would come over to his side.

"It is ready," Kalan told him.

"Then use it," Meliadus growled. "Use it on the troops manning the walls."

Kalan nodded and his Serpents trained the weapon. Kalan stepped forward and seized a great lever. He turned his masked face to the lurid skies as if in prayer, then he pulled the lever down.

The machine trembled. Steam rose from it. It rumbled

R–8   113

and quivered and roared and from the trumpet grew a gigantic, pulsing green bubble that gave off intense heat. The thing broke loose from the muzzle of the weapon and began to move slowly down towards the walls.

Fascinated, Meliadus watched it drift, watched it reach the wall and settle upon a score of warriors. With satisfaction he heard their screams break off as they writhed in the hot, green stuff and then vanished completely. The ball of green heat began to roll along the wall, gobbling its human prey until suddenly it burst and green liquid began to boil down the sides of the wall in viscous streamers.

"It has broken. It does not work!" Meliadus yelled in rage.

"Patience, Meliadus," Kalan shouted. His men were repositioning the weapon by a few degrees. "Watch!" Again he pulled down the lever, again the machine shook and hissed and slowly another gigantic green bubble formed at its snout. The bubble drifted to the wall, rolled over another group of men and rolled again. This one rolled longer until there was hardly a warrior left on the wall when it eventually burst.

"Now we send them over the wall," Kalan chuckled and pulled the lever once more. This time he did not wait. As one boiling green bubble left the muzzle, he would bring another into being until at least a score of the things had drifted over the walls and into the courtyard beyond. He worked furiously, totally absorbed in his work, as the machine shuddered and hissed and threw off its almost unbearable heat.

"That mixture will corrode anything!" Kalan yelled excitedly. "Anything!" He paused for a moment to point. "Look what it is doing to the walls!"

Sure enough the viscous stuff was eating its way into the stone. Huge pieces of highly decorated rock fell into the street below, forcing the attackers to back off. The mixture ate through the stone as boiling oil might eat through ice, leaving huge jagged gaps in the defences.

"But how will our men get through?" Meliadus complained. "That stuff will not care what it eats!"

"Have no fear," Kalan chuckled. "The mixture only has a potency of a few minutes." Again he pulled the

114

lever, sending another huge green bubble of heat over the wall. As he did so, a whole section of the wall near the gates collapsed completely and when the smoke from the rubble cleared, Meliadus could see that there was now a way through. He was elated.

A sudden whine now came from Kalan's machine and Kalan began to fiddle with the improved controls—leaping about from part to part giving hasty directions to his men.

Taragorm emerged on the roof and saluted Meliadus. "I underestimated Kalan, I see." He moved towards the Serpent scientist. "Congratulations, Kalan."

Kalan was waving his arms and screaming with pleasure. "You see, Taragorm! You see! Here—why don't you try it. You merely depress this lever."

Taragorm gripped the lever in both hands, his clock mask turning to look at the wall through which it was now possible to see Huon's troops retreating into the palace itself, pursued by the rolling spheres of death. But then suddenly from the palace a flame cannon roared. Huon's men had at last succeeded in positioning their artillery within the palace itself. Several bolts of fire shot over their heads and others splashed harmlessly on the walls below. Kalan chuckled in triumph. "Those things are useless against my weapon. Aim it at them, Taragorm. Send a bubble—*there*!"—and his finger stabbed towards the windows where the guns were positioned.

Taragorm seemed as absorbed in the machine as Kalan and it amused Meliadus to watch the two scientists playing like schoolboys with a new toy. He felt in a tolerant mood now, for it was obvious that Kalan's weapon was turning the battle in his favour. It was time to join Adaz Promp and lead in the troops.

He descended the steps that took him to the interior of the tower and called for his litter. Once in it, he leaned back comfortably, feeling already a certain sweet triumph.

Then overhead he heard a mighty explosion that shook the whole tower. He leapt from his litter and began to run back the way he had come. As he neared the roof he was driven back by an intense heat and saw Kalan, his mask twisted and buckled, staggering through the steam towards him. "Get back!" Kalan screamed. "The machine exploded. I was near the entrance or I should have been killed. It's spilling my mixture all over the tower. Get away or we'll all be eaten by the stuff."

"Taragorm!" Meliadus said. "What of Taragorm?"

"There can be nothing left of him," Kalan said, "Quickly—we'll have to leave the tower as fast as we can. Hurry, Meliadus!"

"Taragorm dead? And so soon after he had served my purpose?" Meliadus followed Kalan down the ramps. "I had known he would give me trouble after Huon was defeated. I had wondered how to cope with him. But now my problem is solved! My poor brother!"

Meliadus roared with laughter as he ran.

CHAPTER EIGHT

FLANA OBSERVES THE BATTLE

FROM THE SAFETY of her own tower, Flana Mikose-vaar watched the soldiers pour through the breached wall of the palace as the tower that had lately been Meliadus's headquarters toppled, tilted and fell with a crash upon the lower sections of the city.

For a moment she had thought Meliadus destroyed when the tower fell, but now she could see his banner leading the warriors into battle. She also saw the banner of Adaz Promp beside it and knew that Wolf and Hound, traditional rivals, attacked King Huon together.

She sighed. The noise of the battle had intensified and she could find no escape from it. She watched as the flame-cannon vainly attempted to lower and shorten their range, to fire down into the courtyard at the warriors as they rushed towards the great gates of the palace in which the green bubbles had eaten gaping holes. But the artillery was useless. It had been positioned anticipating a long siege and now it could not be moved down in time. A few flame lances fired from the broken gates, but no large artillery.

The sound of the battle seemed to fade, as did the sight of it, as Flana thought again of D'Averc and wondered if he would come. Adaz Promp's news had raised her hopes, for if Hawkmoon were alive then D'Averc was likely to be, also.

But would she ever see D'Averc. Would he die in some skirmish, vainly attempting to resist the might of Gran-bretan? Even if he did not die at once he was destined to live the life of a hunted bandit, for none could ever hope to do battle with the Dark Empire and succeed. She supposed that Hawkmoon, D'Averc and the rest would die on some distant battlefield. They might reach the coast before they were destroyed, but they could not possibly come closed to her, for the sea separated them and the Silver Bridge Across the Sea would not be open to the Kamargian guerillas.

Flana considered taking her own life, but it did not seem worth it at present. When all hope was gone, then she would kill herself but not before. And if she were Queen, she would have some power. There was a slight chance that Meliadus would spare D'Averc, for D'Averc in some ways was the least of Meliadus's hates, though the Frenchman was considered a traitor.

She heard a great shout go up and looked again towards the palace.

Meliadus and Adaz Promp were riding into the palace itself. Victory was clearly in sight.

CHAPTER NINE

THE SLAYING OF KING HUON

BARON MELIADUS RODE his black charger full tilt through the echoing corridors of the King Huon's palace. He had been here many times before and always in humility or apparent humility. Now his snarling wolf visor was proud and a battle-cry roared from Meliadus's throat as he drove his way through the Mantis Guards whom once he had been forced to fear. He struck about him with the great black broadsword that he had wielded so well in Huon's service. He made his horse rear and its hooves, that had trampled the ground of a score of conquered lands, struck down on the insect helms and made necks snap.

Meliadus laughed. Meliadus roared. Meliadus galloped for the Throne Room where the remnants of the defenders were gathering. He saw them at the far end of the corridor attempting to bring up a flame cannon. With a dozen mounted Wolves behind him he did not pause but struck directly at the flame cannon before its surprised operators could move. Six heads flew from their necks in as many seconds and all the artillerymen were dead. Flame lance beams shrieked around the black wolf helm, but Meliadus ignored them. The eyes of his horse were red with a kind of battle-madness and it plunged forward at the foe.

Meliadus pressed back the Mantis Guards, hacking them down and they fell to the floor; they died convinced that he had supernatural powers.

But it was wild energy, the elation of war, that drove Meliadus of Kroiden through the massive gates of the Throne Room to find the few remaining guards in confusion. All possible men had been used to defend the gates. Now as the Mantis warriors advanced cautiously, spears outraised, Meliadus shouted his laughter at them and rode through them before they could move, galloping towards the Throne Globe where earlier he had crawled.

The black globe shimmered and gradually the wizened shape of the immortal King Emperor became visible. The little foetus shape wriggled like a malformed fish, dashing back and forth across the confining globe that was its life. It was undefended. It was helpless. It had never believed that it would need to protect itself against such treachery. Even it, in all its two thousand years of wisdom, had not been able to consider that a Granbretanian noble would turn against his hereditary ruler.

"Meliadus . . ." There was fear in the golden voice. "Meliadus—you are insane. Listen—it is your King Emperor speaking to you. I order you to leave this place, to withdraw your troops, to swear your loyalty to me, Meliadus!"

The black eyes, once so sardonic, were now full of animal fear. The prehensile tongue flickered like that of a snake, the enfeebled, useless hands and feet flapped.

"Meliadus!"

Shaking with triumphant laughter Meliadus drew back his great broadsword and struck at the Throne Globe. He felt a shock run the length of his body as the blade crashed into the globe. There was a white explosion, a wailing cry, a sound of shards falling to the floor and the spattering of fluid against Meliadus's body.

He blinked his eyes, expecting to look down upon the twisted, tiny frame of his slain King Emperor, but he saw nothing but deep blackness.

His laughter changed to a scream of terror.

"By Huon's Teeth! I AM BLIND!"

CHAPTER TEN

THE HEROES RIDE OUT

"THE FORT BURNS well," said Oladahn, turning back in his saddle to look for the last time upon the garrison. It had contained a force of Rat infantry but now not one lived save the commander who would take his time in dying for the citizens of the town had crucified him on the scaffold where he had crucified so many of their husbands, wives and children.

Six mirror helms now looked forward to the horizon as Hawkmoon, Yisselda, Count Brass, D'Averc, Oladahn and Bowgentle rode away from the town at the head of five hundred Kamargian flame lancers.

Their first encounter since leaving Kamarg had been a complete victory. With surprise on their side they had wiped out the skeleton garrison in less than half an hour.

Feeling little elation, but with no sense of exhaustion, Hawkmoon led his comrades on towards the next town where they had heard they might find more Granbretanians to kill.

But then he reined his horse as he saw a rider galloping towards them and realised that it was Orland Fank, his battle-axe bouncing on his brawny back.

"Greetings, friends! I have some news for you—an explanation. The beasts have fallen upon each other. There is civil war in Granbretan. Londra itself is the main battleground with Baron Meliadus in arms against King Huon. Thousands have been slain so far."

"So that is why there are so few here," Hawkmoon said, removing his mirror helm and wiping his forehead with a silken kerchief. He had worn armour so rarely in the past months that he had not yet got used to the discomfort. "They have all been recalled to defend King Huon."

"Or to fight with Meliadus. It is to our advantage, don't you think?"

"I do," Count Brass broke in gruffly, his voice a little more excited than usual, "for that means they are killing each other and evening the odds a little in our favour. While they battle, we move swiftly to the Silver Bridge, crossing it and reaching the very shores of Granbretan herself! Luck is with us, Master Fank."

"Luck—or fate—or destiny," Fank said lightly, "call it what you will."

"Then had we best not ride swiftly to the sea?" Yisselda said.

"Aye," Hawkmoon said. "Swiftly—to take advantage of their confusion."

"A sensible idea," Fank nodded. "And being a sensible man myself, I believe I will ride with you."

"You are most welcome, Master Fank."

CHAPTER ELEVEN
NEWS OF SEVERAL SORTS

MELADIUS LAY GASPING on the stretcher as Kalan bent over him probing at his blind eyes with his instruments. His voice was a mixture of pain and fury. "What is it, Kalan?" he groaned. "Why am I blind?"

"Simply the intensity of the light released during the explosion," Kalan said. "Your sight should be restored in a day or so."

"In a day or so! I need to see. I need to consolidate my gains. I need to make sure that there are no counterplots hatched against me. I need to convince the other barons to swear loyalty to Flana now and then to find out what Hawkmoon is up to. My plans—my plans—are they to be all destroyed!"

"Most of the barons have already decided to support your cause," Kalan told him. "There is little they can do. Only Jerek Nankenseen and the Flies represent a serious threat and Brenal Farnu is with him—but Farnu virtually has no Order left. Most of the Rats died in the early fighting. Adaz Promp is even now chasing Rats and Flies from the city."

"No Rats left," said Meliadus, suddenly thoughtful. "How many dead in all, d'you think, Kalan?"

"About half the fighting men of Granbretan."

"Half? Have I destroyed half our warriors? Half our strength?"

"Was it not worth it for the victory you have won?"

Meliadus's blind face stared up at the ceiling. "Aye —I suppose so . . ."

Now he sat upright on the stretcher. "But I must justify the deaths of those who fell, Kalan. I did it for Granbretan—to rid the world of Hawkmoon and the scum from Castle Brass. I must succeed or, Kalan, I cannot justify weakening the Dark Empire's fighting force to such a degree!"

"Have no fear on that score," Kalan told him with a faint smile, "for I have been working on another of my machines."

"A new weapon?"

"An old one, made to work again."

"What is that?"

Kalan chuckled. "The Machine of the Black Jewel, Baron Meliadus. Hawkmoon shall soon be in our power again and the power of the Black Jewel will eat his brain."

A slow, satisfied smile now crossed Meliadus's lips. "Oh, Kalan—at last!"

Kalan pressed Meliadus back against the stretcher. He began to rub ointment on the baron's blind eyes. "Rest now and dream of your revenge, old friend. We shall enjoy it together."

Kalan looked up suddenly. A courier had entered the small room. "What is it? What news?"

The courier was panting. "I have come from the mainland, your excellency. I have news of Hawkmoon and his men."

"What of them?" Again Meliadus rose up from the stretcher, the ointment dripping down his cheeks, careless that a minion should see him unmasked. "What of Hawkmoon?"

"They ride for the Silver Bridge, my lord."

"They plan to invade Granbretan?" Meliadus was incredulous. "How many men have they? What is the size of their army?"

"Five hundred horsemen, my lord."

Meladius began to laugh.

CHAPTER TWELVE

THE NEW QUEEN

KALAN LED MELIADUS up the steps towards the throne which now replaced the sinister Throne Globe. On the throne sat Flana Mikosevaar in a jewelled heron mask, a crown upon her head, the robes of state upon her body. And before Flana Mikosevaar kneeled all those nobles loyal to her.

"Behold," Meliadus said in a voice that boomed roughly and proudly through the vast hall, "your new Queen. Under Queen Flana you will be great—greater than you have dreamed. Under Queen Flana a new age will bloom—an age of laughing madness and roaring pleasure, the sort of pleasure that we of Granbretan hold dear. The world shall be our toy!"

The ceremony progressed, with each baron in turn swearing his allegiance to Queen Flana. And when at length it was finished, Baron Meliadus spoke again. "Where is Adaz Promp, Chief Warlord of the Armies of Granbretan?"

Promp spoke up. "Here I am, my lord, and I thank you for the honour you do me." This was the first time Meliadus had mentioned that Promp was rewarded with command over all the other commanders, save Meliadus himself.

"Will you report how the rebels fare, Adaz Promp?"

"There are few left, my lord. Those Flies we have not swatted are dispersed and their Grand Constable, Jerek Nankenseen, is dead. I slew him myself. Brenal Farnu and the few remaining Rats have bolted into holes somewhere in Sussex and will soon be flushed out. All others have united in their loyalty to Queen Flana."

"That is satisfactory, Adaz Promp, and I am pleased. And what of Hawkmoon's laughable force. Does it still progress towards us?"

"So our ornithopter scouts report, my lord. They will soon be ready to cross the Silver Bridge."

Meliadus chuckled. "Let them cross. Let them come at least half the distance, then we shall wipe them out. Kalan, how do you manage with the machine?"

"It is almost ready, my lord."

"Good. Now we must set off for Deau-Vere to welcome Hawkmoon and his friends. Come, my captains, come."

And Meliadus was led back down the steps by Kalan and along the hall until he came to the great gates—the gates that were guarded not by Mantis warriors, but by Wolves and Vultures. Meliadus regretted he could not see them and thus savour his triumph the more.

After the doors had closed behind him, Flana sat frozen on her throne and thought of D'Averc. She had tried to speak of him to Meliadus, but he had not heard her. Would he be killed? she wondered.

She thought, also, of what had befallen her. Alone among the nobles of Granbretan, save Shenegar Trott, she had read many old texts, some of which were legends and alleged histories of the years before the Tragic Millennium. She believed that whatever became of herself and Meliadus that she now presided over a court entering its last stages of decadence. The wars of expansion, the internal strife—all were signs of a nation in its death throes, and though that death might not come for another two hundred years, or five hundred, or a thousand, she knew that the Dark Empire was doomed.

She prayed that something better would emerge to take its place.

CHAPTER THIRTEEN

"WHAT DO YOU SEE?"

MELIADUS HELD THE reins of his herald's horse. "You must not leave me, boy. You must tell me what you see and I must plan the battle accordingly."

"I will tell you, my lord."

"Good. Are the troops all assembled?"

"They are, my lord. They await your signal."

"And is that cur Hawkmoon in sight yet?"

"Figures have been sighted riding towards us across the Silver Bridge. They will ride directly into our ranks, unless they flee."

Meliadus grunted. "They will not flee—not Hawkmoon —not now. Can you see them yet?"

"I see a flash like silver—like a heliograph signal— one—two—three, four—five—six. The sun makes them shine so. Six silver mirrors. I wonder what it can mean?"

"The sun on polished spears?"

"I think not, my lord."

"Well, we shall soon know."

"Yes, my lord."

"What now?"

"Now I see six riders, my lord, at the head of a mass of cavalry. Each rider is crowned with flashing silver. Why, my lord, it is their helmets that shine! Their helmets!"

"Are they well-polished, then?"

"They are helms that cover their faces. I—I can hardly bear to look upon them, they are so bright."

"Strange. Still, doubtless the helmets will break quickly enough beneath our weapons. You have told them that Hawkmoon must be taken alive but they can kill the rest?"

"I have, my lord."

"Good."

"And I told them what you said—that if Hawkmoon

should clutch at his head and begin to act strangely that they should tell you at once."

"Excellent." Meliadus chuckled. "Excellent. I shall have my vengeance, either way."

"They have almost reached the end of the bridge, my lord. They have seen us but they are not stopping."

"Then give the signal to charge," Meliadus said. "Blow your trumpet, herald," he said.

"Are they charging, herald?"

"They are, my lord."

"And what now? Have the armies met?"

"They have engaged, my lord."

"And what is happening?"

"I am—I am uncertain, my lord—what with the flashing of those helmets and some—there is some peculiar red light spreading over the scene—there seem to be more men in Hawkmoon's army than we at first thought. Infantry—and some cavalry. By Huon's Teeth—I beg your pardon, my lord—by Flana's Breasts! They are the strangest warriors I have ever seen!"

"What do they look like?"

"Barbaric—primitive—and yet so fierce! They are driving into our forces like a coal through cream!"

"What? It cannot be. We have five thousand troops and they have five hundred. All the reports confirmed that number."

"There are more than five hundred, my lord. Many more."

"Have all the scouts lied, then? Or are we all going mad. These barbarian warriors, they must have come with Hawkmoon from Amarehk. What now? What now? Are our forces rallying?"

"They are not, my lord."

"What are they doing, then?"

"They are falling back, my lord."

"Retreating? Impossible!"

"They appear to be falling back rapidly, my lord. Those that live."

"What do you mean? How many remain of our five thousand?"

"I would say about five hundred infantry, my lord, and a scattered hundred of cavalry."

"Tell the pilot of my ornithopter to make the machine ready, herald."

"I will, my lord."

"Is the pilot ready to fly, herald?"

"He is, my lord."

"And what of Hawkmoon and his band? What of the men in the silver helms?"

"They are pursuing what remains of our force, my lord."

"I have been deceived in some way, herald."

"As you say, my lord. There are many dead. But now the barbarian warriors slaughter the infantry. Only the cavalry escape."

"I cannot believe it. O, curse this blindness! I feel as if I dream!"

"I will lead you to the ornithopter, my lord."

"Thank you, herald. No, pilot—to Londra. Hurry. I must consider fresh plans!"

As the ornithopter beat its way up into the pale blue sky, Meliadus felt a great silver flash pass across his eyes and he blinked, looking down. And he could see. He could see the six flashing helmets the herald had mentioned, he could see the slaughtered legions that he had known would destroy Hawkmoon's force, he saw the remains of his cavalry scurrying wildly for their lives. And he heard the distant laughter that he recognised as belonging to his most hated enemy.

He shook his fist. "Hawkmoon! Hawkmoon!"

Silver flashed as a helmet turned to look upward.

"No matter what tricks you use, Hawkmoon, you will perish by the night. I know you will. I know!"

He looked again, seething as Hawkmoon laughed on. He looked for the barbarians who had routed his soldiers. But he could not see one.

It was a nightmare, he thought. Or had the herald been in league with Hawkmoon? Or were Hawkmoon's barbarians invisible to his eyes?

Meladius rubbed at his face. Perhaps the blindness, so recently left him, was still troubling him in some obscure form. Perhaps the barbarians were on another part of the field.

But no, there were no barbarians.

"Hurry, pilot," he called through the sound of the metallic wings flapping at the air. "Hurry—we must return to Londra as fast as we can!"

Meliadus began to think that Hawkmoon's defeat was not going to be as easy as he had guessed. But then he remembered Kalan and the Machine of the Black Jewel, and he smiled.

CHAPTER FOURTEEN

THE POWER RETURNS

SLIGHTLY OVERAWED BY their victory in which they had lost only twelve killed and twenty slightly wounded, the six removed their mirror helms and stared after the retreating horsemen.

"They were not expecting the Legion of the Dawn," Count Brass smiled. "Unprepared, they were startled and could hardly resist. But they will be better prepared by the time we reach Londra."

"Aye," Hawkmoon said, "and there is no doubt that Meliadus will put a good many more warriors in the field next time." He fingered the Red Amulet about his throat and glanced at Yisselda who was shaking out her blonde hair.

"You fought well, my lord," she said. "You fought like a hundred men."

"That is because this amulet gives me the strength of fifty men and your love gives me the strength of another fifty," he smiled.

She laughed lightly. "You never flattered me so during our courtship."

"Perhaps it is because I have come to love you even more than before," he replied.

D'Averc cleared his throat. "We'd best camp a mile or two on, away from all this death."

"I'll tend to the wounded," Bowgentle said and turned his horse back to where the Kamargian cavalry were grouped, squatting beside their horses and talking among themselves.

"You did well, lads," Count Brass called back. "It is like the old days, eh? When we fought across Europe! Now we fight to save Europe."

Hawkmoon started to speak and then gave a terrible shriek. The helmet fell from his grasp and he pressed both hands to his head, his eyes rolling in pain and horror. He swayed in his shadow and would have fallen had not Oladahn caught him.

"What is it, Duke Dorian?" Oladahn asked in alarm.

"Why do you cry, my love," Yisselda said, dismounting swiftly and helping Oladahn support him.

Through clenched teeth and pale lips Hawkmoon managed to utter a few words. "The—the—jewel . . . The Black Jewel—it—it is gnawing at my brain again! The power has returned!" He swayed again and fell into their arms, his limbs swinging loosely and his face a terrible white. As his hands fell away from his head they could see that he spoke the truth. The Black Jewel was crawling with life once more. It had regained its lustre and it shone with malevolence.

"Oladahn, is he dead?" Yisselda cried in panic.

The little man shook his head. "No—he lives. But for how long, I cannot tell. Bowgentle! Sir Bowgentle! Come quickly."

Bowgentle hurried up and took Hawkmoon in his arms. This was not the first time he had seen the Duke of Köln thus. He shook his head. "I can try to work a temporary remedy, but I have not the materials that I had at Castle Brass."

In panic, Yisselda and Oladahn, and later Count Brass and D'Averc watched Bowgentle work. And at last Hawkmoon stirred, opening his eyes.

"The jewel," he said. "I dreamt it was eating my brain again . . ."

"So it will if we cannot find a way of blocking it soon," murmured Bowgentle. "The power has gone for the moment, but we do not know when it will return again and in what force."

Hawkmoon hauled himself to his feet. He was pale and could hardly stand. "We must press on, then—to Londra while there is time. If there is time."

"Aye, if there is time."

CHAPTER FIFTEEN

THE GATES OF LONDRA

THE TROOPS WERE massed outside the gates of Londra as the six riders mounted the crest of the hill at the head of their cavalry.

Hawkmoon, ill with pain, fingered the Red Amulet. It was that alone, he knew, that was keeping him alive, that was helping him fight the power of the Black Jewel. Somewhere in the city Kalan was operating the machine that fed life to the jewel. To reach Kalan he had to take the city, had to beat the multitude of warriors that, with Meliadus at their had, now awaited them.

Hawkmoon did not hesitate. He knew he could not hesitate, for every second of his life was precious. He drew the rosy Sword of the Dawn and gave the order to charge.

Gradually the Kamargian cavalry topped the hill and began to thunder down on the force that was many times their number.

Flame lances spat from the Granbretanian ranks and were answered by the fire of the Kamargians. Hawkmoon judged the moment right and flung his swordarm skyward. "The Legion of the Dawn! I summon the Legion of the Dawn!" and then he groaned as the pain filled his skull and he felt the heat of the jewel in his forehead. Yisselda beside him had time to cry out, "Are you all right, my love?" but he could not give an answer.

And then they were in the thick of the battle. Hawkmoon's eyes were so glazed with pain he could hardly see the enemy, could not tell at first if the Legion of the Dawn had materialised. But there they were now, their rosy auras lighting the sky. He felt the power of the Red Amulet fill him as it fought the power of the Black Jewel and he felt his strength gradually returning. But how long would it last?

Now he was in the middle of a mass of fear-crazed

horses, striking about him at Vulture helmeted warriors who bore long-handled maces with heads like the stretched claws of hunting birds. He blocked a blow and struck back, his great sword cutting through the warrior's armour and into his chest. He swung in the saddle to take another foe in the neck, ducked a whistling mace and stabbed its owner in the groin.

The fight was noisy and the fighting hot and hysterical. The air stank of fear and Hawkmoon had soon decided that this was the worst battle he had ever fought for, in their shock at the appearance of the Legion of the Dawn, the Dark Empire warriors had lost their nerve and were fighting wildly, had broken their ranks, had lost their commanders.

Hawkmoon knew that it was to be a messy fight and one in which there would be few left alive at the end. He began to suspect that he would not see the finish, for the pain in his skull was growing stronger again.

Oladahn died unseen by his comrades, lonely and without dignity, hacked to pieces by a dozen war axes wielded by Pig infantry.

But Count Brass died in this manner:

He encountered three barons. Adaz Promp, Mygel Holst and Saka Gerden (the latter of the Order of the Bull). They recognised him not by his helm, which was plain save for its crest, but by his body and his armour of brass. And they rode at him in a pack—Hound, Goat and Bull—with their swords raised to chop him down.

But Count Brass, looking up from the body of his last opponent (who had slain his steed and thus left the count on foot), saw the three barons riding down on him and took his broadsword in both hands and, as their horses reached him he swung the sword, cutting the legs of the horses from under them so that each baron was flung forward over his horse's head and landed in the churned mud of the battlefield, whereupon Count Brass dispatched Adaz Promp in a very undignified position in the rear, lopped off the head of Mygel Holst as the Goat Baron begged to be spared, and by this time had only the Bull, Saka Gerden, to deal with. Baron Saka had had time to get to his feet and take

134

a decent fighting stance though he shook his head several times as Count Brass's mirror mask blinded him. Upon seeing this, Count Brass ripped off his silver helm and threw it to one side, displaying his bristling red hair and moustache in all its pride and battle-anger. "I took two in an unfair manner," growled the count, "so it is only fair to give you the chance to slay me."

Saka Gerden charged like the fierce Bull of his Order and Count Brass sidestepped him, bringing his sword around in a swing that split Saka Gerden's helm down the middle and split Saka Gerden's skull, also. As the baron fell, the count smiled and a spear was driven completely through his neck by a Goat rider. Even then Count Brass turned, wrenching the spear from his assailant's grasp, and flung his broadsword to catch the Goat in the throat, thus giving as good as he had received. That was how Count Brass died.

Orland Fank saw it happen. He had left the party before the battle but had joined them later and had done considerable damage with his battle-axe. He saw how Count Brass died. It was at about the moment when the Dark Empire forces, lacking three of their leaders, began to regroup closer to the gates and were only stopped from retreating behind the gates by Baron Meliadus who was most fearsome in his black armour, his black Wolf helm and his great black broadsword.

But then even Baron Meliadus was pressed back as Hawkmoon, Yisselda, D'Averc, Bowgentle and Orland Fank led their few surviving Kamargians and the strange, dirge-calling Legion of the Dawn, against the beasts of Granbretan.

There was no time to close the gates before the heroes of the Kamarg had entered the city and Baron Meliadus realised that he had estimated Hawkmoon's power correctly and then, over confident, had under-estimated it. He knew there was nothing for it but to bring up as many reinforcements as possible and get Kalan to find a way of increasing the power of the Black Jewel.

But then his heart lifted, for he saw Hawkmoon sway in his saddle, his hands going to the silver helm, saw the strange man in the bonnet and the chequered breeks, grasp him and then reach behind him for the roll of cloth attached to his saddle.

Fank murmured to Hawkmoon. "Try to listen, man, will you? It is time to use the Runestaff. Time to bring out our standard. Do it now, Hawkmoon, or you'll live less than a minute more!"

Hawkmoon felt the power gnawing at his brain like a rat in a cage, but he grasped the Runestaff as Fank handed it to him, raised it high in his left hand and saw the waves and rays begin to fill the air around him.

Fank yelled: "The Runestaff! The Runestaff! We fight for the Runestaff!" And Fank laughed and laughed as the Granbretanians fell back in fear, so demoralised now that, in spite of their numbers, Hawkmoon already felt the victor.

But Baron Meliadus was not prepared to be the conquered. He screamed at his men. "That is nothing! It is only an object! It cannot harm you! Forward, you fools—take them."

Then they rode forward with Hawkmoon swaying in his saddle but managing to bear the Runestaff aloft through the gates of Londra and into the city where still there were a million men to stop them.

Now, as if in a dream, Hawkmoon led his supernatural legion against the enemy, the Sword of the Dawn in one hand and the Runestaff in the other, guiding his horse with his knees.

The press was so solid as Pig and Goat infantry tried to tear them from their saddles, that they could hardly move at all. Hawkmoon saw one of the mirror-helmed figures fighting valiantly as a dozen beasts dragged it from its horse and he feared it was Yisselda. Energy flooded into him and he turned, trying to reach his comrade, but another mirror-helmed horseman was already there, hacking about it, and he realised that it had not been Yisselda in peril but Bowgentle and that Yisselda had come to his rescue.

But to no avail. Bowgentle disappeared and the weapons of the beasts, of the Goats and the Pigs and the Hounds, rose and fell above his body until eventually one held aloft a bloodied silver helm—held it aloft only for a moment, for then Yisselda's slim sword had sliced off the wrist so that blood fountained from the arm.

Another searing charge of pain. Kalan was doubtless increasing the power. Hawkmoon gasped and his vision again dimmed, but he managed to protect himself from the weapons whistling around him, managed to hold up the Runestaff still.

As his vision cleared for the moment, he saw that D'Averc was leaping his horse through the Granbretanians, his sword whirling in all directions as he cut a road through them, evidently bound in a definite direction. Then Hawkmoon realised where D'Averc was going. To the palace—to reach the woman he loved, Queen Flana.

And this is how D'Averc died:

D'Averc managed somehow to reach the palace which was still in the condition it had been in after Meliadus had taken it, so he was able to ride through the breach in the wall and dismount at the outer steps to run at the guards on the door. They had flame lances. He had only a sword. He flung himself flat as the flames shrieked past his head, rolled over to take cover in a ditch cut by the green fluid from one of Kalan's bubbles and found a flame lance there which he poked over the edge and used to cut down all the guards before they could know what had happened.

D'Averc sprang up and began to run through the tall corridors, his boots echoing loudly. He ran until at last he came to the doors of the Throne Room where a score of guards saw him and turned their weapons upon him, but he used his own flame lance again and cut them down, being singed only slightly in his right shoulder. He pushed open the doors a crack and looked into the Throne Room. A mile away was the dais, but he could not see if Flana sat on it. Otherwise the hall was empty.

D'Averc began to run towards the distant throne.

And he shouted her name as he ran. "Flana! Flana!"

Flana had been day-dreaming on her throne and looked up to see the tiny figure advancing. She heard her name taken up by a thousand echoes in the huge hall. "Flana! Flana! Flana!"

And she recognised the voice but thought that she had probably not yet woken up.

137

The figure came closer and it had a helmet that shone like polished silver, like a mirror. But the body—was the body not recognisable.

"Huillam?" she murmured uncertainly. "Huillam D'Averc."

"Flana!" The figure wrenched off its mask and flung it from him so that it clattered across the great marble floor. "Flana!"

"Huillam!" She stood up and began to descend the steps towards him.

He opened his arms, smiling with joy.

But they never touched in life again, for a flame beam descended like a stroke of lightning from a gallery high above and burned off his face so that he screamed in agony and fell to his knees, burned into his back so that he slumped forward and died at her feet while she sobbed great, strangled sobs that shook her body.

And a voice from the gallery called in great self-approval. "You are safe now, madam."

CHAPTER SIXTEEN

THE FINAL FIGHT

THE DARK EMPIRE forces were still swarming from every rathole in their maze city and Hawkmoon noted with despair that the Legion of the Dawn was getting thinner. Now when a warrior was slain another did not always take his place. Around him the air was full of the bitter-sweet scent of the Runestaff and the strange patterns in the air.

Then Hawkmoon saw Meliadus and as he did so a wave of pain gnawed again at his brain and he fell from his horse.

Meliadus dismounted from his black charger and walked slowly towards Hawkmoon. The Runestaff had fallen from his hand and the Sword of the Dawn was only loosely held.

Hawkmoon stirred, groaning. Around him the battle still raged, but it did not seem to be anything to do with him. He felt the energy leaving him, felt the pain increasing, opened his eyes and saw Meliadus approaching, the helm snarling as if in triumph. Hawkmoon's throat was dry and he tried to move, tried to reach the Runestaff which lay on the cobbles of the street.

Meliadus said softly. "Ah, Hawkmoon, at last. And you are in pain, I see. You are weak, I see. My only disappointment is that you will not live to see your ultimate defeat and Yisselda in my power." Meliadus spoke almost with pity, with concern. "Can you not rise, Hawkmoon? Is the jewel eating your brain behind that silver mask of yours? Shall I let it finish you, or shall I give myself that pleasure? Can you answer, Hawkmoon? Would you care to beg for mercy?"

Hawkmoon grabbed convulsively for the Runestaff. His hand went around it and tightened. Almost immediately power seemed to flow into him—not much, but enough to enable him to stagger to his feet and stand there swaying. His body was bowed. His breathing came in great panting sobs. He stared blearily at Meliadus as the Baron raised his sword to finish him.

Hawkmoon tried to raise his sword, but could not.

Meliadus hesitated. "So you cannot fight. You cannot fight. I grieve for you, Hawkmoon." He reached forward. "Give me that little staff, Hawkmoon. It was upon that that I swore my oath of vengeance upon Castle Brass. And my vengeance is almost complete now. Let me hold it, Hawkmoon."

Hawkmoon took two staggering paces backward, shaking his head, unable to speak for the weakness in his body.

"Hawkmoon—give it to me."

"You—shall—not—have—it . . ," croaked the Duke of Köln.

"Then I shall have to kill you first." Meliadus raised his battle blade and then the Runestaff suddenly pulsed with brighter light and Meliadus stared full into his own Wolf-helmed eyes as Hawkmoon's mask reflected his image back. It startled Mediadus. He hesitated.

And Hawkmoon, drawing further energy from the Runestaff, raised his sword knowing that he had only enough strength for one blow and that that blow must slay the man who stood transfixed before him, mesmerised by his own image.

And Hawkmoon brought up the Sword of the Dawn and he brought it down again and Meliadus gave a great, agonised cry as the blade bit through his shoulder bone and down into his heart. And his last words, which came with his last painful breath, were:

"Curse the thing. Curse the Runestaff! It has brought ruin upon Granbretan!"

And Hawkmoon collapsed to the ground knowing that now he would die without a doubt. That Yisselda would die and that Orland Fank would die, for there were hardly any warriors left and the Dark Empire soldiers were many.

CHAPTER SEVENTEEN

THE SAD QUEEN

HAWKMOON AWOKE IN alarm, staring full into the Serpent mask of Baron Kalan of Vitall. He sprang upright on the bench, groping for a weapon.

Kalan shrugged, turning to the group of people who stood in the shadows. "I told you I could do it. His brain is restored, his energy is restored, his whole foolish personality is restored and now, Queen Flana, I would beg your permission to continue with what I was doing when you interrupted me."

Hawkmoon recognised the heron mask. It nodded once and Kalan shuffled away into the next room and carefully closed the door. The figures stepped forward and Hawkmoon saw with joy that one of them was Yisselda. He hugged her in his arms and kissed her soft cheek.

"Oh, I feared that Kalan would trick us in some way," she said. "It was Queen Flana who found you, after she had ordered her troops to cease fighting. We were the last alive, Orland Fank and I, and we thought you dead. But Kalan brought you back to life, removed the jewel from your skull and dismantled the machine so that none may ever fear the power of the Black Jewel again."

"And what did you interrupt him in, Queen Flana?" Hawkmoon asked. "Why was he so disgruntled?"

"He was about to kill himself," Flana said flatly. "I threatened to keep him alive forever if he did not do what he did."

"D'Averc?" Hawkmoon said, puzzled. "Where is D'Averc?"

"Dead," said the sad queen in the same flat voice. "Slain in the Throne Room by an over-zealous guard."

Hawkmoon's joy turned to gloom. "And are they all dead, then—Count Brass, Oladahn, Bowgentle?"

"Aye," said Orland Fank, "but they died for a great cause and they freed millions from slavery. Until this day

Europe has known only strife. Now perhaps people will seek peace, for they can see where strife leads."

"Count Brass wished for peace in Europe more than anything," Hawkmoon said. "But I wish he could have lived to see it."

"Perhaps his grandson will see it," Yisselda said.

"You need fear nothing from Granbretan as long as I am queen," Flana told them. "I intend to have Londra destroyed and make my own town of Kanbery the capital. The wealth of Londra—which is almost certainly greater than all the wealth of the rest of the world—shall be used in rebuilding the towns of Europe, in restocking the farms, of making good, as best we can, the damage we have done." She drew off her mask, revealing that great, sad, beautiful head. "And, also, I shall abolish the wearing of masks."

Orland Fank seemed sceptical, but he said nothing. "The power of Granbretan is broken for ever," he said, "and the Runestaff's work is done here." He patted the bundle under his arm. "I'm taking the Sword of the Dawn, the Red Amulet and the Runestaff itself into safe-keeping, but if there should ever come a time, friend Hawkmoon, when you have a mutual need to rejoin each other, then you shall rejoin each other, I promise."

"I hope the time does not come, Orland Fank."

Fank sighed. "The world does not change, Dorian Hawkmoon. There is merely the occasional shift in equilibrium and if that shift goes too far in one direction, then the Runestaff attempts to right it. Perhaps the days of extremes are over for a century or two? I do not know."

Hawkmoon laughed. "But you should — you are omniscient."

Fank smiled. "Not I, my friend, but that which I serve —the Runestaff."

"Your son—Jehemiah Cohnahlias . . ."

"Ah, there's the mystery even the Runestaff will not answer." Fank rubbed his long nose and looked at them over it. "Well, I'll say farewell, what's left of you. You fought well and you fought for justice."

"Justice?" Hawkmoon called after him as he left the room. "Justice? Is there such a thing?"

"It can be manufactured in small quantities," Fank told him. "But we have to work hard, fight well and use great wisdom to produce just a tiny amount."

"Aye," Hawkmoon nodded. "Perhaps you are right."

Fank laughed. "I know I am right." And then he was gone. And his voice came back to Hawkmoon with just one last observation. "Justice is not The Law, it is not Order, as human beings normally speak of it; it is Justice —Equilibrium, the Correction of the Balance. Remember that, Hawkmoon. Remember it."

Hawkmoon put his arm around Yisselda's shoulders. "Aye, I will," he murmured. "And now we return to Castle Brass, to make the springs flow again, to bring back the reeds and the lagoons, to bring back the bulls and the horses and the flamingoes. To make it our Kamarg once more."

"And the power of the Dark Empire will never threaten it again," smiled Queen Flana.

Hawkmoon nodded. "I am sure of that. But if some other evil should come to Castle Brass, I shall be ready for it, no matter how powerful it shall be, or in what form it will come. The world is still wild. The justice Fank spoke of has hardly been manufactured at all. We must try to see that we can make a little more. Farewell, Flana."

Flana watched them leave and she was weeping.

THE END